1775

by

Keith Korman

ALSO BY KEITH KORMAN

Swan Dive

Archangel

Secret Dreams

Banquo's Ghosts (with Rich Lowry)

End Time

Teahouse of the Hidden Moon (update edition)

A Conservatarian Press Publication

ISBN: 978-1-957586-43-4

1775

A Novel of the War for Independence

This book is a work of historical fiction. People, places, events, and situations are sometimes drawn from history, but more often the product of the writer's imagination. The writer has striven to retain as much historical accuracy as possible.

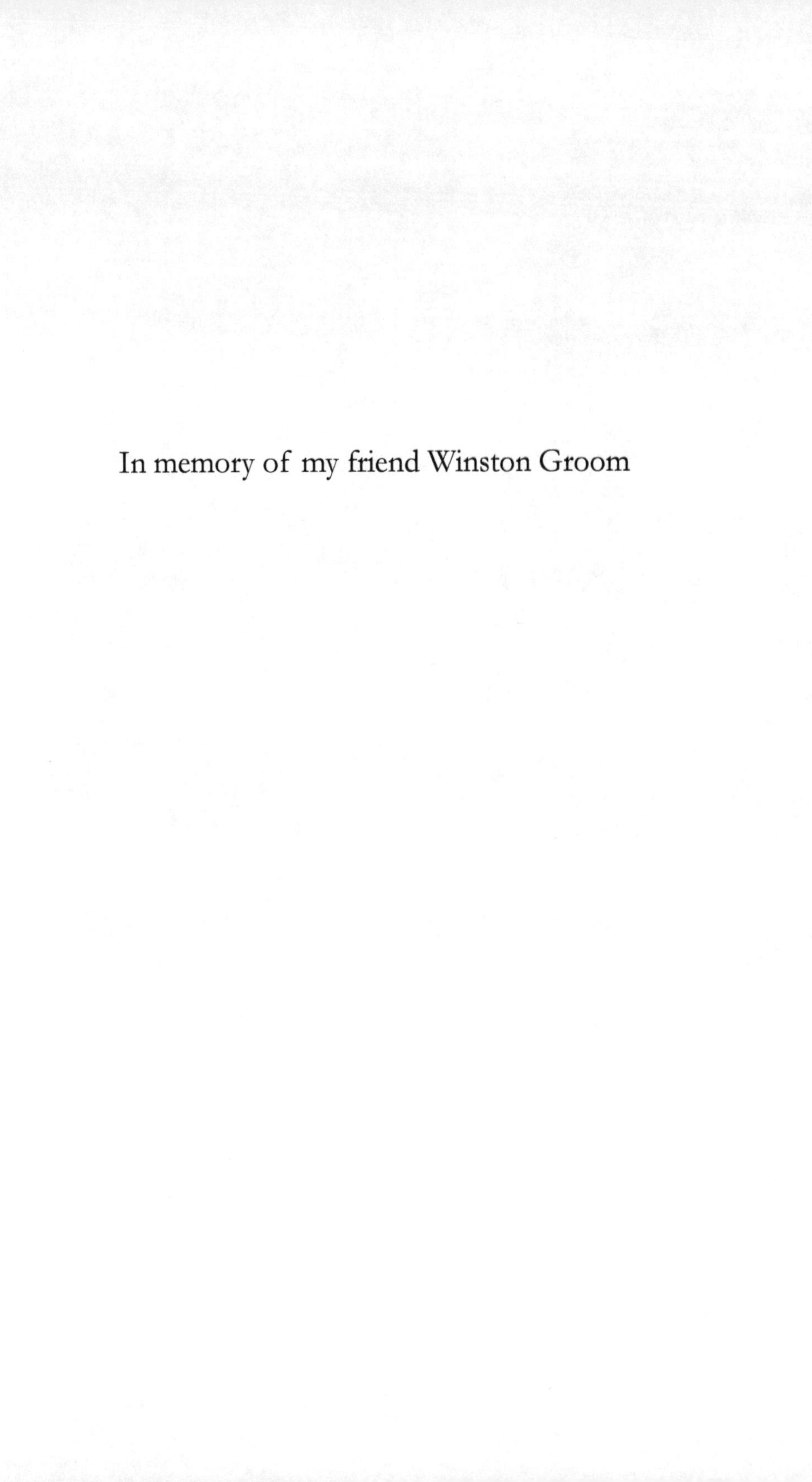

In memory of my friend Winston Groom

Contents

Chapter One: The Green Dragon 13
Chapter Two: Lanterns in the Dark 17
Chapter Three: Muck 27
Chapter Four: The Lonely Scone 35
Chapter Five: Boston Cannonaded 39
Chapter Six: How Had It Come to This? 45
Chapter Seven: Intolerable 57
Chapter Eight: Midnight March 63
Chapter Nine: Alarmums 69
Chapter Ten: Road to Folly Pond 75
Chapter Eleven: Midnight Ride 83
Chapter Twelve: Buttered Rum 89
Chapter Thirteen: Dark March Dark Thoughts 93
Chapter Fourteen: Skirmish 103
Chapter Fifteen: The Bridge 113

Part II

Chapter Sixteen: House of Dead Eyes 121
Chapter Seventeen: March or Die 133
Chapter Eighteen: The Porcupine 139
Epilogue: Happy Christmas 145

There comes a time in every man's life that he turns from his own,
and wants to join the other—

If only in the hope of ending the fight for good.

– Vetus Lupus

Chapter One: The Green Dragon

Boston. April 18th, 1775. 8:30 PM.

Spy hunting is a dirty business, and the local tavern its gritty arena.

Nothing good happens after midnight.

As for the spy hunter himself: a lonely, unhappy man, ever subject to the beck and call of his social betters. Whether he be a sailing privateer, a land-bound lawyer, a bespectacled accountant – a butcher, a baker or even a candlestick maker. Always at some fop's beck and call. The spy hunter can be a gentleman in difficulties or just a soldier following orders. In nearly every case, rub a dub dub – the man is driven hither and yon by a lord who never soils his hands, never muddies his boots or hears the drooling nonsense spoken at a tavern's final call. While tobacco smoke hung in wavy curtains from wall to wall, along with the reek of unwashed men – their mumbling voices barely stirring the stinking air.

The sorry likes of:

"She never loved me."

"Cow and calf, both colicky."

"A roof shingle cracked and now there's a leak."

Embers burned in a fireplace that stopped drawing before ten at night and always seemed to need a rest before clearing the air again. Pipe stem bits littered the floor, bitten off and spat out like broken teeth. Sloughs of sawdust pushed about by shuffling feet, clotted with clumps of horse dung. The whole place nothing but a smokey spittoon, upended and forgotten.

Of The Green Dragon's genteel clientele, some drunkard, named Hollenbeck – a drover – had pissed himself in his chair and fallen asleep in it. Perhaps The Green Dragon would be spared the inevitable bout of fisticuffs at closing.

Lieutenant Moreau of His Majesty's Royal Marines stared bleakly across the worn tables and wobbly benches and wondered dismally if he'd ever return to Mayfair and fair Meg again.

Moreau, fourth son of an earl in the poor sheep-bitten district of Yarmouth and as close to penniless as you could get without losing the spare change in your pocket. Meg and he locked eyes that day in Kew Gardens, and no greater words of love could ever be spoken, no promise or pledge ever made. All that remained were haggles over finances, accounts and pedigree. Little of which helped Lieutenant Moreau's cause. Even less when his regiment dispatched by ship to Boston to oversee the troublesome colonials.

Nothing worse than promises delivered to a woman and then never kept. We shall gain your father's consent, we shall marry, we shall live on my military pay and your endowment from your first marriage, and eventually my commission shall return me to London.

Yet nothing in Boston led anywhere near connubial bliss, back to Mayfair or Meg. Only to this crusty tavern across an ocean and within smelling distance of the harbor, its fisheries, and wharfs steeped in rancid cod guts and crushed oyster shells.

Back in The Green Dragon Lieutenant Moreau watched two of his men, Bates and Cummins steadily drinking. Both marines out of uniform but fooling no one as to their identity. The muttonheads were hoping to overhear some good tidbit of intelligence. Rebel spies abroad that April night up to no good. Ever since the great black ships arrived stuffed to the gills with red-coated soldiery, the comings and goings of every colonial was suspect, to be regulated, watched and otherwise overseen. The black doings of colonial rustics, hiding weapons, gunpowder, food, caches of muskets and pistols, anything to fight a war. Find them, arrest them and if lucky, tie them to their horses to bring them back alive to Boston for summary justice.

And both soldiers perfectly useless to the task. Not that two sober sots, johnny-on-the-spot would've done any better. A month ago, Lieutenant Moreau had told his superior, the Major, that their quarry – the Silversmith – had abandoned The Green Dragon. That Mr. Smith – the Silversmith – was nowhere to be found and ceased using this public house, this smoky spittoon, either for operations or conspiracies. The Green Dragon being Mother Hubbard's Cupboard since the advent of Lent.

And in any case, the colonists' most infamous rebel, Revere, was at home for the evening this pleasant April night. Not prowling the unpredictable countryside or instigating trouble in Boston proper. As far as Moreau knew the rebels' engraver had not stirred from his house on 19 North Square all night. And he told the Major as much. No doubt the Major posted men nearby just to be sure. But the Major would have none of Lieutenant Moreau's extra intelligence from this useless drinking hole. Pertinent information on the order of – the many sharpshooters prowling the countryside. That every mile inland was another step into hostile territory. That an angry man or woman waited in every house or behind every tree. That the deeper you marched into boggy Massachusetts the harder it would be to retreat. To these concerns the Major seemed oblivious.

Day in and day out, as far as the Major was concerned – it was Rebels in the Taverns. Rebels in the Streets. Rebels once and forever. Except there were no rebels in The Green Dragon, as Lieutenant Moreau could plainly see, and the night's work amounted to his two men getting stupid-drunk until closing time.

If they stayed that long.

The rebels were "out there" somewhere just waiting – and sooner or later the Kings' Men would find them – and not in the King's favor either. But in the locals' favor with loaded powder and ball, both seen and unseen.

Moreau watched the large ale keg beside him drip heavy drops from a leaky bunghole into a pewter pail. drip-drip-drip A liquid metronome marking irrelevant time. Either the spigot or the hole must be warped. The innkeeper labeled the faulty keg holding rebel ale "The Clap" and sold whatever came out of it for half price.

Was it worth the trouble for Lieutenant Moreau to have his drunk men bring a dozen gallons or so back to the deserted barracks for Major Mitchel?

Compliments of the house?

But there was no cart available for the task and Lieutenant Moreau wasn't the kind of officer to make the men under his command lug six gallons each on a milkmaid's yoke.

As if to settle the question of The Clap once and for all, a uniformed corporal banged through the front door of the ale house, spotted Lieutenant Moreau and came directly over to his table. The last shreds of anonymity went down the drain. The corporal unclenched a damp, crumpled bit of paper.

Dispatch from the Major.

Come at once. Boats. Crossing.

That settled it. The King's men were to march upcountry this very night. Some would go south down Boston Neck and others in boats, across the Charles. In either case, marching the King's men up and down the countryside in dead of night was thirsty work. Perhaps they should expropriate a cart from some clodhopper and bring the ale after all. Even The Clap might be welcome somewhere on the way out or on the way back.

For tonight they were to go slogging into the backcountry.

Lieutenant Moreau knew the rough plan. Standing orders the same as always. A chase-tail under orders from Governor Thomas Gage.

Six hundred Marines under Lieutenant Colonel Francis Smith's command, and two hundred Marines under Major John Mitchel as advance party to march on Lexington. And it went unsaid, that orders, like all orders – on strictest of confidence – managed to escape their keepers in the command tent and circulate widely to the blissful ignorance of nearly everyone involved. Moreau himself had spied the orders on Major Mitchel's camp desk:

> *You will march with the utmost expedition and secrecy. You will seize and destroy all the artillery, ammunition, provisions, tents, small arms and all military stores whatever … But you will take care that the soldiers do not plunder the inhabitants or hurt private property.*

So, if a tavern was a place where nothing good happens after midnight, then a forced march down dark roads into hostile territory before midnight, in search of more spies and their supplies couldn't lag far behind.

What's worse, yet another rumor had gone around that the whole command – would on no account fire, nor even attempt it without orders.

Pathetic. Hopeless. Imbecilic.

Lieutenant Moreau rose from his table. High time to join the marching band down by the Commons. A churned-up muddy patch smelling of horse dung and urine, with dozens of tents staked into the ground like a white pox in a sward that would never turn green. Lieutenant Moreau kept away from it as much as he was able. No point in either dirtying himself or his horse in the greasy muck that was Boston Commons.

If the boats forded the Charles River in a timely fashion, they'd be across the water and walking the old Bay Road before ten tonight. Leaving the rest of the night to achieve a sore derriere, a tired mount, and an infantry man's sore feet till dawn.

The lot of them, under orders to hold fire.

Chapter Two: Lanterns in the Dark

Boston. April 18th, 1775. 8:30 PM –
Clark's Wharf – Revere Silversmith Shop

The rectangular windows in the Silversmith shop reflected Pith Street and Clark's Wharf. Every morning Mister Cuddy, the shop steward, wiped the windows with clean rags. Over the course of a day, wharf traffic, sea sweat, and lantern smoke dulled the glass. By dusk you could write your name on the panes in harbor grime.

That evening, some provincial Tory wag had come along and finger-scrawled an insult:

Farmer Georgie's Catamite.

The King's butt-boy. But who cared? What matter nasty names – when the dangling rope was always handy?

The shop steward rubbed out the graffiti with the side of his hand. The window glass panel itself was thick with bubbles and veins – a milky pane designed more for light than sight. And hardly anyone looked up from their work benches when the smith was busy with the tinker's clinks of bending silver.

After the day's work was done, little if anything moved along the waterfront.

An old man pushed a handcart past shop windows and vanished around a corner. His straight back showed the two-wheeled cart empty of cod or mussels or oysters, all sold by now.

Out in the bay, smack and schooner masts gently tipped back and forth, a buoy bell dinged with a forlorn sound and a three-quarter moon rose over the black hulk of a royal man 'o war.

The Crown's 70-gun HMS Somerset anchored in the harbor – an immense ship, a sleeping Gargantua, tied soundly to its mooring chain. The scudding clouds made the huge ship appear in moonlight and disappear into the black. A floating bastion, a blockhouse of immeasurable strength which suddenly loomed out of the dark when the moon shone its face. Then vanished again as the clouds veiled the light. A few lanterns burned in the great ship, a few in the rigging, one or two on deck, the faint glow of a candle in the captain's cabin.

But the cannon ports were closed, a massive black hulk. Leviathan asleep. Yet the message clear – from its anchorage in the harbor, the Man o' War could shell every road, pound every building and blast every Christian soul in Boston to Kingdom Come.

Three other Royal warships rested at anchor. Each ship a dark, impending threat. Each with cannon, shot and powder, each able to scour the bay and shoreline. Mister Cuddy wondered how any people could resist such coiled, waiting power?

The shop steward looked toward the clack of hobnailed boots, the footfalls sounding the approach of the town's lamplighter. The man tramped up the street, going about his business of banishing the night. Lighting the lanterns at every corner and dock post and doorway. Lamp after lamp. Finally reaching the lantern over the Silversmith sign.

Everyone knew the lamplighter, a fellow with the improbable name of Dobbin Fish. Dobbin paused as he lit the lantern beside the shop, taking his time under the sign that read:

REVERE and SON

With the lamp lit, a pale light fell upon the shop steward's African face. Mister Cuddy's dark skin was almost blue, with tribal facial scars across his cheeks. Narrow raised chevrons, slanting down. A formidable countenance.

"Up late, Mister Cuddy?" the lamplighter asked.

"I am, Mister Dobbin Fish. Up late for reasons known and unknown. And all known to you."

"I understand," Dobbin replied. Then glanced down the wharf-way. The spire of Christ Church rose above the clustered buildings of the North End. Tallest building in sight.

"Well, there's the answer." The spire dark, black as sin. No lanterns, no lights. No signal.

"Can't make up their minds," Mister Cuddy said.

"But they gotta come one way or another." Dobbin Fish said. The lamplighter turned away from the silversmith shop and opened another creaky lantern glass hanging on a wharf piling.

"But whichever way they come, across the bay or down the pike, them regulars be too late. The word gone forth. Everyone knows. Them red coat regulars miss their aim. An' I told him straight to his face as I'm lighting the lamps down by the common."

"Told who, Mr. Fish?"

"Oh, one of them red generals, the long-faced one with the big nose. They call him Earl Percy, I think. He ask me, 'What aim are we missing, lamplighter?' An' I answers, 'why dem cannons out there cross the river, your lordship – they be moved the minute the muster in the common happen. An' I see his face turn white, an' he say, 'thank you, lamplighter. An' he hitch up his sword belt and run for the Province House where the bigger general is waiting in his command house. An' a minute later a dozen regulars burst out the door to stand on the wharf by the pike out of town."

Cuddy could see a handful of regulars along the wharf front. Milling about at the start of the road inland, as if waiting to do something. Guarding the little boats from anyone who thought of making a crossing to the mainland.

"But them red soldiers assemble too late, too late – the word gone forth into the countryside – hither and yon – that a passel of regulars are marching out coming for guns and powder. Looking for trouble."

Cuddy let this sink in. No doubt Mr. Paul and others had already made good their escape from Boston proper. And in a few moments Dobbin Fish the lamplighter had moved on to other lamps, clinking open the lamp latches and lighting the wicks.

Mister Cuddy checked one last time inside the shop. Dark within, nothing amiss. The work benches clean, the stools stacked, the floor swept. The endless rows of tools – hammers, tongs, gravers, bezels, along with anvil heads, stakes, pliers, snips, files and scribers – sitting on shelves or hanging from pegs. The tools adorned every spare wall of the shop like regiments of soldiers waiting at attention. Even in the dark, the shop steward saw nothing missing, nothing out of place. For he had cleaned and put them away himself.

Mister Cuddy shuttered the shop windows.

With noisy ring of keys, he threw the deadbolt and with a final rattling twist locked the door. Better git to Mr. Paul's house.

The dark buildings on either side passed quietly. As he ducked into Love Lane, lights in the houses came on, candles burning on windowsills. Funny how lights burning behind the glass bewildered the eyes and kept you from seeing too much inside. When he passed a metal hitching post, his fingers touched the clammy iron ring and it rattled. A familiar touch.

A ring of iron.

How well he knew it. In a rush, the Slave Years returned to his mind with the tang of the ocean on the beach, and the swell of the waves rolling onshore.

Slave Years.

The Port of Ouidah, the nation of Dahomey. His one and only home, but what he came to despise like no other place on earth. The coast of Africa. How old was he then? Fourteen?

He remembered all too clearly.

Their cousins from another tribe came into the village just before dawn. Cuddy awakened to the sound of thunder. Firesticks boom-boom and belching smoke, the cousin tribe slaughtered half the men and took the rest. The grownups they shackled neck to neck by a tree limb yoking each, man or woman to the next. The boys and girls they dragged by a noose – hands tied. Stumbling, falling, neck wrenched at the end of a leash.

From the green jungle inland, they were marched down to the shore. Miles they walked, through thorn and brush, feet stumbling, trying not to trip, or bang a rock – finally arriving at a beach, the sand strewn with great lanky ribbons of seaweed. Under the shade of palm trees, something he'd never seen before, great casks made of wooden slats. Barrels. They called them barrels. Those barrels he would soon know as Rum Barrels. The Devil Rum.

Across the rippling blue and white crests, he saw the big ships for the first time. He never imagined anything that big could sit upon the water. Blistering heartless hulks, tall masts, little colored flags fluttering in the wind. The wooden bulks sat upon the ocean, solidly in the swell – awaiting what? Somehow, he knew – *awaiting him.*

For three long days he watched the ships rock patiently offshore. Watching from behind the wooden bars of an enclosure. A ribbed box. A cage. Speaking no language but his own, he did not know they called this prison, a barracoon. Knowing no language but his own, he knew only the names his parents and grandparents gave him.

His given name from his parents, was "Unexpected."

While his grandparents gave him the others.

Another name came from his father's father, "Not Look Like Him."

And his third name from his mother's mother, "Only She Knows."

Even at 14, never quite sure what all that meant, but as his skin was twice as dark as Papa, so when people called him Unexpected! He began to get the idea ...

Not look Like Him. Only She Knows.

And as he was unexpected, nobody would miss a bastard from that stricken village. And once sold into the dank hold upon a silver sea, nobody would ever miss the village. When the boats returned, they'd just march further inland, ever inland looking for more human horseflesh to pack onboard.

Once behind the barracoon, the enclosure's bars, he knew only the heat of the day, hunger and the burning thirst between dollops from the great casks, called Rum. As the days progressed, and the slavers brought more people onto the beach, the dead went from one dead to two dead, to three dead, the smell of the carcasses everywhere. Odd how faces of men and women you recognized and knew for all your life, when they died went through a change.

At first you knew them. The face without any expression and you knew who they were, Big Toothy or Curvy Little Woman. Then the bloat began, and their bodies swelled up like a rotted pig, big and fat, and every face turned big and fat and each looked alike, big, and round and fat with eyes swelled shut. And you could only tell those you knew – from the others – by their wraps or cloths or pretty things. Curvy Woman wore a shell necklace, Big Toothy an earring. Until they smelled so bad, they needed to be moved from the barracoon.

The white men made them drag the bodies from the enclosure under point of their firesticks. The reluctant ones who wouldn't budge from the cage, they called "cuddies." Later, he found out the word meant 'Donkey' in Scottish, but at the time the word only meant pain.

"Get that cuddy."

"No, not that one, the other cuddy."

"Yes, that cuddy."

"The big, stupid Cuddy. Beat him if he won't move."

Everyone beaten like donkeys.

But not all these human donkeys moved. Some cuddies were already dead.

Some too sick to move. Yet the insensible or dead were beaten as well. Beaten in order to find out if they were faking, if there was any life left in them. For many pretended they were dead in the empty hope they'd be left behind.

For the truly dead cuddies, the dead men, they dumped on the beach, covered with sand, that soon became encrusted in flies … the barracoon door locked again.

And time for more Rum.

The Rum made them all stupid, then desperate for water. And the slavers rolled out barrels of water. To tempt them. To make them do exactly what they wanted. But from the beach to the ship's hold to the colonies the name cuddy stuck. Human donkey. All of them named Cuddy.

Once on board no longer called by his proper name, Unexpected – now from this moment to forever –

Cuddy. The human donkey of the new world.

Branded as such for all to see.

Bound and gagged again, a black man slaver with a missing tooth took a knife, showed him the knife to his face. While two others held him, the toothless slaver put the knife in a bed of embers. And when the knife turned red, the men put his head in a wooden clamp. Toothless sliced three slashes on each cheek with the red-hot knife to mark him property.

The mark of the ship they were to travel on, the Slaver Bark, Three Seals. Making the three hatch marks on his cheeks. Three on each side, his head held in a wooden vice as the flesh sizzled at each touch. And the smell of burnt flesh – yes, that of sheep, of lamb. Somewhere, someone close by was screaming. Screaming at the top of his lungs.

Himself.

Then a blackness and he knew no more.

Unexpected awoke to see sailors on the beach. Several small boats were drawn up on shore; the last pulling up to the sand shipped its oars and ground to a ha Lieutenant Then a crowd of white men marched up the blinding white strip of land, the first white faces he had ever seen, led them all around the Forgetting Tree. A single palm stump, shattered at the top by cannon fire – without leaves or coconuts, standing alone at the edge of the beach.

Frantic with thirst, the white men showed him more water, gave him a sip, then for the whipping. Nine times the men marched Cuddy nèe Unexpected and the others around the stump. The Whites shouting, "You never come back! You never come back!"

Not for the last time, he would hear those exact words, but whipped all the same, they all where, whipped around the Forgetting Tree. Bound and gagged and driven round and round until exhausted, ready to drop, they were ready to leave their past behind. Then the little boat, then the large boat, then climbing the hull, then down into the hold. More shackles. More whipping, more Rum, and the sweat of the others. And four weeks of darkness.

There'd be other scars added later. But the damp crust of rusty iron, the clammy sea sweat around your neck, the swaying ship, every human animal stench filling your head to bursting. An hour shackled to a wall an eternity, but four weeks shackled to a wall – damnation. Damnation. Excrescence.

Damnation. Excrescence.

He learned those two complicated words at the end of the voyage. In Key West. When the slaver bark Three Seals finally came to port. Expropriated by the Colonies. The cargo never sold at auction in Jamaica. But arrived in the New World, free as a bird. Innocent as original sin. Without a stitch of clothes. Not even a loincloth.

A drum was brought up from the cargo hold and a black cabin boy they knew as Lil' Dick – who fed them slop and water – began to dance on the quarter deck. They squinted in the terrible sunlight, cowering, heads under arms as Lil' Dick sang:

Hey nonny-nonny, Hey nonny-nonny

Enter his gates, and Thank Him Muchly,

For he Made Us, He Made Us –

So come along home, come along home,

And let Thos grand Folks up there,

Thos gran' Folks up there

Adore you! Adore you!

A group of gaily dressed women with shawls and parasols tittered among themselves, along with the good citizens of Key West, seigneurs and servants alike (no, he didn't know the word for parasol then) – the crowd stood upon a great veranda on a building looking down at the ship's deck. Fistfuls of puffy clouds slowly sailed across a hopeful sky.

And as the black men and women and children came out in filth and shackles and very, very naked, there were gawps and gasps from the crowd overhead.

A few spectators rushed to and fro, collecting every shawl and bit of cloth at hand from any man or woman who would part with it. Bits of clothes passed hand and hand, down to the stinking men and women to clothe their nakedness. But first the bath. Great tubs of sea water poured over every one of them and barrels of fresh water with gourds passed down. The thirst slaked, the thirst –

While Lil' Dick danced by the quarter deck rail, crying, "You be free! You be free!"

Later, he learned the slaver ship, Three Seals had been intercepted before it reached Jamaica. Brought to the free port of Key West, and yes, no slave would go to auction down in Jamaica –

Cuddy stopped in his tracks. The dank streets of Boston harbor surrounded him like a soft moist cocoon. All that was thirty years passed. Back in clammy Boston, Christ Church spire rose overhead. Two lights in the bell tower in the spire flickered to life. Like two eyes, the great lanterns burned into the night. And you could see the message from every point along the shore and within the town. Two lanterns.

The message clear.

The British troops in search of rebel spies and supplies would come across the water, starting at the Commons thence onto at the broad section of the Charles River, parts muddy and other parts dry at Low Water.

Cuddy reached Mr. Paul's house in North Square. As he crossed the flagstones his eyes never left the spire. Surely his master saw the lights too. Surely everyone would. Redcoats too. Two white eyes staring into the night. Staring long enough for the world across the river to see. Shining out into the darkness for the briefest minute. And then as if the tower read his thoughts of caution and alarm, the two lanterns flickered out and vanished as if they'd seen enough.

Mister Paul's front door wasn't locked. Cuddy didn't knock but tried as quietly as possible to enter. Across the square he heard a soldier on guard clear his throat and spit. The Grenadier had seen him and was letting him know it.

If Mr. Paul had been there he'd be listening in the dark – the Silversmith hearing the door creak open – then close – footsteps in the hall. Footsteps in the house, knowing it was Mister Cuddy his shop-boy. And always telling his hired man the same thing, whispering, "Saw the soldiers in the house across the way. Seem to have been there forever. Night and day."

"I know, Mister Paul, the Grenadier said hello."

But no Mr. Paul was waiting there. The vacant front room yawned at him, the house empty and Cuddy's footsteps creaking floorboards without answer from within.

No Mr. Paul.

Hah! British regulars watching an empty house.

General Gage had quartered the soldiers across the street for months; long enough to forget what their job was about. Keeping tabs on the underhanded comings and goings of Traitor Revere. The King's men, sitting comfortably behind partly drawn curtains, feet up, taking turns by the fire and the rum, lazy as the fatted calf. A maidservant brought them dinner every evening, then vanished home.

Nothing different tonight than any other night – except the two lanterns in the Spire. And the fact that the General had sent extra men hither and yon to prevent anyone from leaving Boston proper. The Robin Red Breasts not only missed their aim but missed their mark entirely. If Mr. Paul wasn't in the house, it meant he'd already made good his passage. Fled.

So, if the signal meant anything to the King's men in the house across the way, they made no show of it. Besides, what could they do? Change marching orders when the King's soldiers were already mustering in the commons? They'd have to send a runner round the bend in The Charles, half a mile along the south shore to Back Bay. Then the runner would have to get a sign-off from the General. Who might or might not be disposed to any last-minute nocturnal change. Too late for all that. The Brits' mustered longboats were waiting on the strand, waiting for the tide to lift them off the bar. They'd be rowing across the Charles come perdition. And once across – what difference would it all make?

Maybe none at all. Maybe quite a bit. Depends on where you caught the tide.

Time. And tide. The water was coming in.

And if Mr. Paul wasn't in the house, if the lobsters across the street were watching an empty box. Mr. Paul had gotten out okay. All quiet, no alarums. Even if General Gage had sent his extra men to lockdown Boston proper, they'd missed their mark. Too late, too late to stop the warning.

The vision of Mister Paul under guard in his house was just a fantasy and quietly faded to thoughtless smoke. His entry into Revere's house the merest Rus to keep the Royal guard's attention where it did no harm.

For Cuddy saw the escape not an hour before.

Mr. Paul used a tiny skiff tied up in shadow, close by in a narrow nameless slip, not far from Christ Church. The small boat barely made a ripple in the bay for the moon to catch. Barely an hour before, from the shadow of a lampless streetcorner, Cuddy watched the three men get into the boat. Mr. Paul and two watermen, a boat builder and a shipwright – the large and the small of it, pushed off a short quay, dipping their oars into the black ink of the Charles. Their shoulders covered in dark cloaks, when the clouds overran the sky, the skiff itself disappeared. "Check on the shop before you retire, Mister Cuddy," came the Silversmith's voice. "Be back in the morning. See you then."

The tide slowly came in, pushing up the Charles River. Here in the narrows the river mouth shrank to a mere few hundred yards, and the incoming tide drove the skiff along with almost no effort, the boat gliding across the surface like a water-bug skating across a pond. Oarlocks wrapped in rags so they didn't clack. The Cambridge shore came closer and closer, dip after dip of the wet blade. Stealth and silence and black water covering all. The dark spire of Christ Church showed no signal, but suddenly the moon unveiled her face as if blessing them both, the men and the bell tower.

Then hid herself again as if to say, cloak yourselves now, so no one sees –

Chapter Three: Muck

Back Bay, 10 PM

A bare mile south, Lieutenant Moreau held the tiller of his longboat command. Eighteen Marines pulling oars, grunting with effort and to little effect. And God knows, who exactly they were.

That was one of the problems – enlisted men, non-commissioned officers and commissioned officers, professional soldiers all – had been thrown together hodge-podge, into units that had the cohesion of curdled milk. Yes, they'd done some marching and some bivouacking. But since disembarking their troop ships, none really knew each other. The commanding officers were mostly volunteers and attached to each unit at the last minute. "You go here, you go there," Command from Province House told their officers. And Lieutenant Moreau complied, there was nothing else to be done. Eighteen nameless men in his longboat and his two non-commissioned officers worse than useless. The eighteen men looking darkly at the sergeant and corporal wondering what on God's green earth allowed them a hangover when the rest had to remain upright and sober.

What to say? Life was unfair and the army even more so.

His two inebriated men, Bates and Cummins, looked green around the gills. That last tankard of The Clap from the Green Dragon's leaky cask had gone down too sweetly and now did its work. In the lean-forward stroke, Bates managed to vomit over the side, to the general groans of the men.

"Quiet!" Lieutenant Moreau ordered. "The next man who discharges his gorge will spend a week in the blockhouse."

Cummins missed a stroke and wretched across the gunwales, getting some in the bilge.

"Except Bates and Cummins, who were on special assignment."

A general guffaw quickly stifled. That sounded like, serves them right.

"Pass the man a water flask," Moreau ordered. The two hungover soldiers drank greedily but the stink of their bile seemed to drift along with the boat. Despite the stink, the men liked their Lieutenant, as the Lieutenant often contrived to see them fed and well bedded. And often out of his own pocket when need arose. Moreau knew all too well, that loyalty purchased was loyalty all the same. Even if he didn't know all their names.

He toyed about making moniker tags for the uniforms and sewing them on the breast of each man, but who in this redcoat army who bought or inherited their commissions wholesale would see the usefulness of that?

Damn few.

Lieutenant Moreau's longboat was one in an extended line of His Majesty's conveyances making for the riverbank or the landing at Lechmere in Cambridge. And the boats were making a hard go of it, struggling against the current. Unlike the tide by Charleston and Boston's North end, this same current sluiced southwestwards against His Majesty's longboats. With every stroke the rowers struggled to cross a much wider part of the Charles northwards towards the mainland. Some command tent toad had forgotten to consult a tide table. A mile up you could glide across effortlessly on a southernly slant, like a leaf on a pond.

But down by Back Bay, a mere mile or so around the curve of the town, in a longboat sculling north, an oarsman was pulling against that same incoming tide. And they were inching forward, going almost nowhere with a mighty effort.

Nearly thirty feet long, the sturdy, solid craft could brave nearly any swell at sea, but for this damn crossing they'd been better off ferrying men to shore with all their equipment, in wooden shoes. Easier to go by land, march down Orange street, cross the causeway of Boston Neck and through the South Battery into Roxbury. Whether by day or night, an impressive sight. Men a' foot, showing the commoners, the Provincials, both rebel and loyalists that fearsome animal, the marching red dragon of the British Light Infantry.

But no, the command toads wanted stealth and secrecy and above all quiet. Lieutenant Moreau was reminded of that line in Richard II – 'Let's march without the noise of threat'ning drum.'

The Bard's play about a struggle for supremacy – Lord Bolingbrook, Duke of Hereford, displays the might of his men for the skulking King, retreated to a ruined castle. The Duke to march his men before the assembled haughty personages gathered among the "rude ribs" the fallen fortification of Richard's redoubt. But to march without the thumping noise of the drum, indeed, to march silently back and forth before the ruined gates, the silent threat of tramping feet and hooves and to await a King's answer on whether there would be war or parley on this day …

Back then, Commanders knew the value of ostentation and display. It saved a lot of blood. And yet, how odd, how damningly close was this play's scene to what the King's Men were about this night.

Close, but not exact. There would be no display, only surreptitious scuttlings in the darker corners of a rude, backward colony. And this wasn't a choice between war and parley, but a moment of sly reckoning over who had the goods on whom.

So, they loaded up the longboats, shoved off and fought the current inch by bloody inch. To make things more difficult, the boats were loaded down with the men's haversacks, water flasks, powder and ball pouch, swords, bayonets, boots, hats, redcoats, salt pork, sea biscuits, and each man wore a blue cloak over all so, letting them blend into the night and the black water.

Not to mention twenty muskets, the old reliable Brown Bess and twenty odd men. Including the weight of the longboat itself, five hundred pounds easy, each filled boat weighed two tons, of goods and human lard. It takes a lot of muscle to move that against a current and without a sail and on manpower alone. After twenty minutes pulling oars the men were soaked to the bandoliers with sweat.

The longboat keel grated suddenly, stuck in some muddy shallow oyster bed or sand bar. This time Moreau's men couldn't stifle the groan. The men rocked the boat, planted their oars to push off the sand bar – while Lieutenant Moreau stood up, jumping up and down at the stern, rocking the vessel. The keel see-sawed and the boat broke free. They saw other longboats in the dark, bouncing up and down as well. Splashing wooden fish.

The Lieutenant's brass gorget rattled at his neck and he cursed the damn thing. A shiny metal plate hanging about your neck, engraved with the Royal Seal of Lion and Unicorn, and of questionable significance. Yes, once upon a time the metal throat armor might have been useful when used in combination with chainmail or breastplate, to turn a dagger in close quarters – but now, just an ostentatious display of rank. The only conceivable use – to glitter in the sun so Regimental Command could spot you in the field through a spyglass when grapeshot mowed you down and you fled in retreat.

As the boat slid through the water now, Moreau dropped the tiller for a moment and unhooked the damn silver thing. Momentarily the Lieutenant considered tossing it into the drink and then just as unceremoniously tucked it in his frock pocket.

As they neared the Lechmere shore their boat ground up against yet another patch of muddy bottom, along a wall of longboats similarly stranded. The shore itself was only a few dozen yards off, and the first wave of longboats clogged and rocked in the deeper inlets as the tide sluiced in. Men struggled over the gunwales, splashing up to their knees and some their hips. They faced a nasty muddy, watery trudge up the bank, only to reach rough fields and the scant shelter of a woody copse.

No road in sight.

Lieutenant Moreau saw these struggles from his spot at the tiller – dozens of men waddling in the mire, holding dear Brown Bess over their heads, then sinking up to their calves as they struggled to shore. His own boatmen shipped their oars and began to strap on their equipment. And Moreau suddenly realized a critical moment had arrived, a command decision.

Make it correctly and his men's day might actually improve, make it badly and things would only get worse. Get to shore fairly dry, or at least muddy, rather than marching with thirty pounds of gear, soaked to the bones.

"Hold!" he called out across the gunwales. His men froze. "Rag! Use your oars, find us solid footing."

Obediently, his two rogues, his two Ding-boys as the rebels would say, grappled with their oars and began to prod about the wet mud bar beside the boat. The rogues grunted as their oar blades went plunk-spoosh into the black water. Sergeant Bates and Corporal Cummins then stumbled round the boat planting their oars into the muck.

First Sergeant Bates, in a whisper "Aye, Leftenant – maybe here!"

"May… be – she's good here." When Corporal Cummins pressed down on his oar, it sank a foot into the mud. When the corporal yanked it out, water flew and doused him on the chops. "May be not so." Another plunk-sploosh. The oar held. The two soldiers found their spot.

"Well Lads, you know what to do," Lieutenant Moreau said quietly.

They did. The two officers removed their leggings, boots and stockings, and put their footwear in their packs. Then donned their packs and bandoliers without rocking the long boat. Sergeant Bates kept the oar but handed his musket off to the corporal. Cautiously the sergeant stepped over the gunwale into about six inches of water. His foot held on the mud, another foot followed. Carefully Corporal Bates followed. Then the other men in the longboat, naked feet padding quietly behind.

The sergeant went ahead using his oar like a blind man's cane, every few steps pressing it into the water to sound the bottom. The riverbank no more than thirty yards away, but not as the soldier marched. No, the Sergeant's pathway, halted, twisted, turned. Each time he found a deep spot, he'd poke around, and around – until he found something firmer. This way, it took forever to get to shore. A meandering, snaking line of plodding men. Dipping their toes in then twisting about to find better footing. And only one man cut his naked foot on a broken oyster shell. Of all the long boats, Lieutenant Moreau's men fared the best.

Better wet feet than mud slop to the gills.

Other platoons were up to their waists, and hips, slogging along up and down the line, some flailing away with their arms, cursing and splashing water like otters. All the while the officers were trying to quiet them, and Lieutenant Moreau realized, at least for now – they'd been lucky. His men had been lucky. The operation had been lucky.

A few dozen rebels with muskets could have cleared the banks of Red Coats in three volleys of shot. But nothing tonight. No rebels hidden in the trees.

They crawled up on shore about the same time as the rest, their naked feet wet, yes, but no more than ankle deep. They'd clean off the mud, dry their damp toes with handkerchiefs or musket rags. And back on go the stockings, the boots and leggings – feet dry and ready for marching till dawn. Lieutenant Moreau's men were the only infantrymen with a hard day of soldiering ahead on this riverbank with dry feet.

As Moreau's men gathered themselves into a presentable troop, Major Mitchel appeared out of the dark on a bay mount. The Major's spotless uniform, leggings and boots meant he'd crossed over some time before and not by way of longboat and mud. The Major's horse, just as spotless must have been this side of the river for quite some time. Major Mitchel gave Moreau's men a long glance down a thin nose, appraising them in light of the other troops' soaked, and bedraggled state. The words came out, flat, indifferent with a touch of snide.

"Afraid of a little wet, Leftenant?"

"Not when it can be avoided, Sir."

The mild rebuke evoked a snort from the Major and the dry observation:

"You're out of uniform, Leftenant. Where's your Gorget?"

"Frock pocket, Sir. So as not to be lost in the water," Moreau replied calmly, suddenly thankful he hadn't tossed it in the drink. The useless silver Gorget glittered for a moment as he fished it out of his pocket. "To be displayed at once."

As if to taunt the popinjay, a cacophony of noise erupted out of the surrounding dark. The peal of bells ringing, shots fired and hoarse cries came at Moreau's men from a morphing mass of rustics hiding in every shadow. Like the savage calls of wild men coming at them from every direction. The countryside already roused and signaling every village and homestead at their arrival.

Alarm and Muster. Lieutenant Moreau knew how it would go now.

The element of surprise totally blown away like a candle in an open window. The cacophony rose and fell and seemed to move on out ahead of them.

The Major sniffed and turned away. Even mounted upon his horse, the commanding officer seemed to strut. Of course, he knew every hillock and copse of trees would have spying eyes as they marched inland. But it didn't seem to dismay him in the least. As if walking into some kind of trap were every soldier's duty to perform.

"You're at the bottom of the pot, Moreau, get them moving. Our precious quarry, the Signifier and the Maltster will have long fled to a squaw's longhouse where we'll never find them. By dawn there'll be nothing left but privy detail. There's another horse for you, up above we brought along. That old nag you ride."

"Belle. Thank you, sir."

"Yes, Belle. Mount her then."

The worst possible outcome – being late with nothing left to do. No heroics, no mention in dispatches, no way to distinguish his command. Worse still, the two rebel worthies, the Signifier and the Maltster could well have fled beyond reach of the King's Men.

Command wanted these two since forever and were just waiting for an opportunity and reason to arrest them. If the two rebels were caught shifting supplies around that would be enough, finding an unloaded musket by the bed would be enough. That fop, John Hancock, known as The Signifier for his fancy signature, was a clever dandy, blockade runner, not to mention wealthy as Croesus. And if he didn't want to be found, he wouldn't.

While the other, Samuel Adams, known as the Maltster. Inheriting his dah's brewery, landing in the lap of commerce, making sour ale, worse than even The Clap – before otherwise becoming a perfect social failure. Uncomely to look at, annoying to listen to, impossible to befriend. Such an ugly duckling should have been easy to spot and grab, but no. Not him neither.

The Major and the whole command had been hunting these phantoms for months to no avail. Along with their rebel supplies left like Hansel and Gretel breadcrumbs which they found with regularity. Digging up one cache after another. Guns, sacks of peas, jerky, pemmican, gunpowder, whale oil, up and down the Bay Road. Sometimes the Provincials moved their swag, sometimes they didn't. As of late the caches were empty; every cache barest bones, meaner than a parson's cupboard. The rebels were keeping their swag some place, the soldiers just didn't know where.

As though every rebel knew the soldiers would be coming. Cannon too. The rebels had been rolling a stolen brass cannon from one locale to another and if the troops could find this one single piece of artillery… the whole expedition would be worth it, even if the Signifier and the Maltster slipped through their fingers.

A few yards off, a line of trees turned into a road. The mixed regiment of Grenadiers, Royal Marines and Light Infantry formed up along road's edge under the eyes of their officers. Each soldier wrapped in a dark blue cloak, some much wetter than others. Some subaltern appeared with the mare, Good Belle, and handed the reins to Moreau. The mare didn't seem put out in the least to be working at this ungodly hour.

Better to walk now than ride. And Moreau saw his own men notice that he walked her by hand. Even without knowing their names he saw their attitude and manners. Favorably impressed, deducing with a single mind they had an officer who shared the hard parts with them.

Shared burden and shared duty made for an extra bond.

A bond that any smart officer would wait to cash.

Wait until that do or die moment when the bacon was in the fire and urge to flee, a raging epidemic.

Back on the road, the men began to move in broken cadence, and Moreau's dark thoughts gave way to the real dark that enveloped them. The dark of night. Better than a blue cloak. Better than any command tent plan.

Chapter Four: The Lonely Scone

15 Miles Inland
Hartwell Tavern, Hartwell Farm
Bay Road 9PM

Another town, another tavern.

The Massachusetts colony was awash in ale and beer. Alehouses, tap rooms, grog shops, planks with tankards and barrels in the street, anywhere to quaff a thirst. Almost every hundred paces in any town, cross a threshold, find a bench and take a draught. Every mile you rode another sign of the Inn waved to you from painted placards showing the rude icons for bread, beer or rum. That is, when bread, beer, and rum could be had.

But this year's British blockade ladled a thin, dreary sauce over everything. The brave lads dumped few dozen crates of tea in the harbor on more than good cause and stirred an implacable tide of men at arms, ships of war, privation, and inconvenience. Royal Troops ensured nothing from the outside came in and nothing from the inside went out.

No rum, no sugar, no rice, no oil, no molases, no cotton, no indigo, no wheat, no tobacco, no –

The good news – yards overflowed with lumber, furs stored by the atticful, dried game and fish plentiful, if tiresome. But when a pair of scissors broke, good luck finding another. When you lost a needle from a pincushion, better hope there's an extra stuck in your bonnet.

And who in the Lord's name grew wheat in Massachusetts? Some hardy souls but the yields were small. Not quite hot enough, not quite flat enough, and a crop could be destroyed in one summer hailstorm. So, they returned to the old staple, baking bread out of corn, instead of white loaves. The barely digestible Johnnycake.

As you bake so shall you brew. Beer out of rye or barley. Whiskey instead of rum. Every tavern bet its livelihood on the fact that thirsty men drink anything, and never complain. Puddles in a cow pasture, duck water from a duck pond. Whiskey from any malted seed or chaff or mash. And every innkeeper poured tankards for men who'd never pass on a slug when the thirst was upon them.

At the early hour of nine in the evening, the Hartwell Tavern rounded their second wind of the night. The sun had set hours ago through a yellow haze of road traffic from passing carts and horses. On windless days, the floating dust on Bay Road hung like a muslin curtain, stirred again and again by wagon, rider or carriage. But by early evening, the dust had settled for good.

Mary Hartwell looked up from her bookkeeping ledger, as one sot staggered out the door and yet another sot staggered in, rubbing shoulders. For a moment the two guzzlers were indistinguishable, tipsy men in knee breeches, frock coats, and cocked hats both cocked askew. Mary Hartwell's sorry-looking bookkeeping ledger showed similar ins and outs, chicken-scratched numbers in marching columns, as many debit lines as credit ones. The first four months of the year had been dismal. If the absence of customers continued, she'd be feeding ale to pigs.

Such was the life of a tavern keep. Ink stains, drunks, ale and pigs.

Husband off with the minute men.

Some even called her the Widow Hartwell. This was not the first night she missed her helpmeet. Not the first night her spouse abandoned the smokey room and tapping the kegs. Not the first time he ignored fetching brew to tipsy men – all for a rebel night's galivanting in the dark. She couldn't remember the last time she'd had her knickers twisted.

Still, she sorely missed him. Then resented him his man's freedom, then missed him again.

Yet there was one new face that stuck in her mind. Floating up from nowhere. And dammit it all, to make matters more confusing – an officer of the King's own.

The chiseled, haunted face of a young lieutenant. One who'd taken the time to shave that morning and with the faint scent of lavender cologne, and not acrid sour of week-old sweat. His scarlet uniform clean, his lace cuffs and ruffled cravat at his throat clean and white. With not even the hint of mud around his boots. A British officer with a Frenchie name, Morel, no Moreau. Yet no free spirit, the man bore a weight and sadness that clung to him like the faint caresses of a long-lost lover. Caresses that would never come again.

A strange longing blossomed in her chest. A deep yearning from out of nowhere – an unbidden vision –

Given the moment (and there was always an opportunity) Mary would lure the handsome man into the dark back of the tavern and lift her skirts. The coy smile, the lifted eyebrow, the silent unmistakable invitation, no man could resist. Invite him to fill her loneliness amongst the empty barrels, hoops and staves. A few moments of ragged breathing and rutting – quickly ending in release and empty sighs. A recovery and straightened bodice, the skirts dropped once more. Not a word spoken, not even their names.

The female heat dissipated as quickly as it came. Nothing fair about a woman on her own, even a married one. For a some moments the woman looked dismally about the smoky tavern, the rough tables, the odd three-legged stools and plank benches. Not half as many bench sitters as she needed to turn a profit.

On umpteen nights the two most respectable customers in her establishment often sat quietly in one corner. The two lovebirds, Maid Mulliken and the handsome Doctor Prescott. Not tonight, alas. She could use their coin, their business.

But even more – lonely Mary could use their radiant heat.

Their affections were contagious. A kind of warm, sensuous glow enveloped the two paramours. And warmed her as well.

While the two hardly spoke… Doctor and Maid would share coffee, and stare over a single scone on a pewter plate between them. Endless nights, they'd sip the coffee and gaze longingly at each other, hardly saying a word and ignoring the lonely scone entirely. Every so often, the two would whisper the occasional word while muleskinners and drovers swigged apple jack and noisily downed tankards – and paid no more mind to the two sweethearts than the potted ferns on the windowsills.

Hartwell's Tavern – as good a place as any for assignation; showing the busybodies the world what respectable courting looked like. Maid Mulliken, smart as she was refined – knew enough to limit a gentleman caller to the front door of her home – as any more familiarity might seem too forward or too intimate. While sober, public "tea times', drinking coffee in a public house could never be construed as other than chaste.

And if the two lovers, Maid and young Doctor found themselves treading in a nighttime meadow on their way home, feet quietly tramping God's green grass, what passed between them then was theirs alone. The townsfolk, their neighbors, travelers and most everyone else approved of the young couple. The youthful fellow was more than likeable in that innocent way men can have before they get ale bellies and miss shaving the gristle under their chins. And Maid Mulliken was a proper young lady. With no flaws to speak of.

However, this long evening, neither Maid Mulliken nor the young doctor appeared at their regular table in their safe corner to ignore their scone. Merely, another dark shadow in a room of shifting shadows. If the two sweethearts lavished attention on each other, the act took place somewhere else. No doubt, young Dr. Prescott was more than willing to oblige his Maiden any venue for a tryst where the lovebirds' hands might twine like the necks of cranes.

Mary Hartwell left off dreams of romance at the noise of their Negro, Sukey, coming in through a connecting door. Sukey lugged two buckets of fresh dishwater, one soapy, one clean. Their servant put down the buckets and wiped her forehead and looked plaintively for help.

"I'm hearing wind in the trees," Sukey said. "There's a mess of comings and goings. Can't you hear it, Missus Mary?"

The tavern keeper left her ledge and began to help with the pails.

"Not a thing. All I'm hearing tonight is the goings not the comings," Mary replied crossly.

If only a few more customers had appeared, maybe she'd turn a profit. But everyone seemed to be somewhere else.

"If you find out where our regular customers are, Sukey – send them back. We need the business."

Chapter Five: Boston Cannonaded

Steeple, Christ Church
10 PM

Mister Cuddy watched his patron's boat slip off into the dusk. The plash of oars dipping into the drink dropped off to silence. Nothing to see in Boston Bay but murk and nothing to hear but the lap of water against the wharfs and the soft gong of a buoy bell. Faint candlelight glimmered from the curtained windows in the surrounding buildings. The moon flickered over the cobblestones for an instant, then hid her face behind a cloudy veil. All Mister Cuddy knew was that Mister Paul wasn't coming back today.

He turned back toward the town.

Overhead, the bell tower loomed like a dark sentinel above the rooftops. The black embrasure of the bell chamber blackest of all; then for a silent moment the shop steward begged God for the light of the lanterns in the high tower once more. As it had been earlier in the evening. It should be two lanterns. Two lanterns, a signal to anyone watching, whether on near shore or across the bay – the soldiers were coming by water. But there was nothing, darkness, only a silent bell tower in a silent church.

Then all at once the sainted light appeared – two flames in two lanterns. The cold light burned in the belfry for a moment, an agonizing moment. And Cuddy froze in place, hands and body up against the nearest building as if terrified someone would catch him staring. Catch him standing there and instantly grasp which side of the troubles he was on.

Arrest him. March him off somewhere cold and dark.

Again, his hand found an iron ring attached to a building, the iron horse hitch covered in sea-sweat, the touch coarse and final.

He looked to the bell tower again, as if to confirm the sight. But there was nothing now, the lights extinguished – no light, no lanterns – and Cuddy took a deep breath. A trick of the eyes, a trick of the mind? No, they'd stagger the signal. On. Then Off. No point leaving them burning indefinitely, just more chance of being discovered.

As if to shake the moment, the shop steward struggled from the clammy wall. A few paces on Cuddy passed a lonely sausage seller closing up his stall and bought four sausages, a small jar of pickled onions, and a few strings of dried green beans. The sausage seller grinned at him, "Thank you, sir!" Nothing better than an unexpected late-night sale. Cuddy put his purchases in a drawstring sack and looked up towards the spire. The lights flickered in the steeple, then vanished. And the blackness returned as if the signal never happened.

Suddenly, the food in the sack felt heavy. More than enough for the men waiting in the church.

The single church door was built under the spire. Cuddy hesitated to knock and looked around – the church dark and silent in an empty street. Three cats appeared out of nowhere, intent on a hunt and chased each other around a corner without making a sound. If anyone gazed from the close-packed houses, or from behind a curtain, he couldn't tell. Cuddy fished a soft rag out of his frockcoat pocket – his handkerchief – and wrapped it around his knuckles. Then knocked softly.

"It's me, Cuddy," he whispered. No answer. Within, the floorboards creaked as footsteps approached the door. The fellow on the other side cleared his throat. The church door sighed open slightly.

"Oh, it's you. So, he's off across the water. Good."

Cuddy pushed through the narrowly opened door. Cuddy marked the figures of three men. A man's shadow retreated toward the pews. Sexton Newman, caretaker of the church. "Lock the door." Cuddy paused to lock it with a dry, final click.

Two other men quietly turned from their seats. Dark figures in dark pews, yet Cuddy knew them. Vestryman John Pulling was the other lantern man who helped the Sexton into the tower. And their lookout, the sturdy Tommy Bernard. Obviously no longer at his post, now that the signaling was done. The two lanterns now extinguished sat in their own pew like any two sober Sunday psalm-singers waiting for the sermon.

"What'd you bring? We're starved."

Without even waiting to see, the men tore into Cuddy's provisions, nearly ripping the drawstring sack from his hands and pawing through it. Sexton Newman seemed in a mighty hurry. He clutched a link of sausage to his breast, naming it with great relish, "Ahhh, Hungarian Yard!" and strode toward a window, drawing up a chair to stand on so he could climb outside.

"No one noticed me leaving Mum's house," Sexton Newman said before he vanished over the windowsill. He meant the Redcoats. "Pray they won't notice me coming back."

The last Cuddy saw of the Sexton that night was the absurd figure of a man's rear end struggling through a half open window clutching a length of Hungarian sausage.

"Close the window before you leave," came his fading voice from outside.

The good Sexton Newman lived at his mother's house and the old biddy had been quartering three British junior officers since the tea got dumped in the harbor. At least the soldiers paid the rent she demanded on time and the spying worked both ways. The British officers were well-situated to detect any Provincial breaking wind and the Biddy Newman heard every bit of scuttlebutt passing between her quartered guests. The worst of it, Biddy Newman was forced to tolerate the redcoats' muddy boots in the parlor.

Back in the church, Vestryman John, their sturdy lookout, rose from his pew, leaving the large lanterns sitting there, pious as any in the congregation.

"We're glad you're going to stay," the Vestryman told Cuddy.

Without waiting for a reply his companion remarked, "If something important happens, at least you'll see it. Take some pew cushions." Cuddy nodded silently. He took several long pew cushions from the benches. Hard boards made his bones ache, and the cushions would make a good mattress. This promised to be a long night.

The Vestryman handed Cuddy a wooden bucket. The necessary.

"Just in case."

And a bottle of precious tea.

In another moment the lord's house was empty except for the church mice. Cuddy went to the belfry stairs clutching his pot, his tea bottle, his food in the drawstring sack, and two long pew cushions under his arm.

At one end of the gallery under the steeple, the pipe organ sat like a sleeping ogre. Cuddy glanced at the perplexing keyboard and pedals with their umpteen choices, confusing beyond measure. Someday I will learn that, he thought. If old Biddy Newman can do it, I can do it. Then scrunched around a narrow gap at the rear of the console to a small door. The narrow stairs to the tower.

That's when he felt the burden and tension of what just happened to the men who'd just left. The Signalers in the Steeple. It came to him in a rush, like all his visions. Seeing and feeling it clearly as if he'd done it himself. The consequences of action. The cause and effect. When the lantern men shone the light from the tower. How it went for them. What they saw – as if he saw it himself. Coming right up his feet, step after step and into his brain.

The stairway creaked under foot, and with each new step he saw how it had gone before. Sexton Newman and Vestryman Pulling had gone up, climbing one by one, just like him. The Signalers in the Steeple ascending in total blackness. Breath short, then gasps rising with each step upwards. The dark, unlit lanterns in their hands, heavier as they climbed. Totally out of breath, as they reached the belfry.

Exertion and Fear.

Had anyone heard them climb? Would anyone see them in the open belfry? Would their lookout below, sing out if troops suddenly arrived? That's right, the Sexton was supposed to come inside again and whisper up the belfry stairs. Would they even hear him up this high? How in God's name would they get out again? They'd climbed a one-way trip to the stockade shackles or a prison barge. Better if they just lit the lanterns and ran off –

Cuddy reached the belfry. The moonlight shone for a moment through the belfry windows, showing the bell, the floorboards, the harbor below. Not long ago, the signalers crouched to light each lamp. The Vestryman and the Sexton. The Vestryman first readied the lanterns, opening their glass doors, not daring a whisper.

Sexton Newman started fussing over his small tinderbox. A round, lidded, tin snuffbox as the base, with the stump of a candle in the holder.

He laid out his firestarter – first the firesteel, then the flint, then the charcloth, then some saltpeter rubbed touchwood. A slight breeze wafted across the belfry. Enough to snuff any flyspeck flame. This would never do.

"Better crouch on the stairway and hand me the lamps, one at a time," one Steeple Man said to the other. They'd closed the narrow door below, so as not to make a draft chimney of the belfry. The Sexton curled his fingers around the halfmoon firesteel. He struck the flint once, a shower of sparks, then again, a shower of sparks on the charcloth. Nothing.

"Damp."

The Vestryman fished a small tube of paper out of his pocket. Gunpowder. He sprinkled some onto the charcloth and the touchwood. The other readied the candle stub.

"All right, if we have to."

This time a scrape and – fisssssss! A little flash. The cloth and wood caught. The Sexton blew softly, the charcoal glowed. He blew again and brought the tinderbox candle to bear – the tiniest flame licked to life.

"Steady now."

The candle lit one lantern wick and then the next. Then he gently blew out the candle. "Ready?"

Carefully the two men climbed the last bit of stairs to the belfry platform. Then placed each lantern on the belfry window ledge. Two lanterns. The message clear – the redcoats would cross The Charles by boat.

"Count it out, John," the Sexton said.

And the Vestryman obliged. Counting slowly to sixty while staring at the minute hand on his pocket watch. "One … two … three …"

The longest sixty seconds anyone had ever lived. Seeming to go on forever, "twenty-two …"

"Thirty five …" God, they were only halfway through. Still no warning of soldiers' approach from their lookout Tommy below. Just a few more seconds, just a few –

"Forty-seven …"

And then finally six and zero and then they were done.

Duly flashed. Duly shuttered. Two lamps, one signal.

One and done.

Lamp doors shut. The darkness returned.

The two men crouched on the belfry landing, their limbs growing cold.

"I hope they saw it."

"If they didn't, the hell with them!"

The two men, done for good, clattered down the stairs from whence they came, lanterns banging against their thighs.

Cuddy's reverie fled like a ghost and the shop steward came back to reality. He placed his cushions carefully and lay himself down. Old bones grateful for the comfort. Long night ahead.

From the tower Cuddy could see the British warships anchored in the harbor; one large vessel sat on the water like a great malevolent colossus – appearing and disappearing into the black as clouds scudded across the moon. The largest of the four, a Man o' War, the venerable HMS Somerset, almost ready for the scrapyard but with 70 guns, the aging bucket an indominable, armed blockhouse.

The others, two ships of the line and an armed schooner, enough guns to devastate the city and the surrounding shoreline half a mile inland. HMS Preston and HMS Glasgow – 50 guns and 20 guns – brought the whole of Boston Town under imminent threat of barrage.

Behemoths ready to unsheathe their guns, prime their barrels, ram home a thousand cannonballs, and let fly a fusillade, a cannonade flattening everything within sight and beyond.

The smallest ship, the war schooner Diana, hovered on the water like an angry wasp, poised to sting anyone or anything the three leviathans overlooked. Four vessels packed to gills with men and steel and gunpowder.

The soldiers they disgorged came ashore like armed marching ants, Achilles' myrmidons – advancing across the countryside. Into every village, every hamlet, into every stable, workshop, factory floor, farm and barn in the colony.

But the hulks now slept at anchor, a silent menace. Their power contained, a drawn fist. A few watch-lights burned on each vessel. But their mute message obvious to all:

We only begged for loyalty and a few pence.

Instead, you murdered and spat on us.

Now you raise the fist of war.

Be Warned.

Be Damned.

We will pound you into dust.

Boston Cannonaded.

Chapter Six: How Had It Come to This?

Steeple, Old North Church
11PM

How had it come to this?

Like all human matters. Born of chaos and confusion. Its worst elements smoldered away for decades. Punctuated by bouts of anger. Lulled to sleep for a bit then rudely awoken by kicks and pummels. Its least harmful elements blown into insanity. Its most harmful elements swelling like a weeping cyst. Symbols over substance. Substance over common sense. Anger and ignorance walking hand in hand through a garden of nettles.

Why is it that all good things take decades to make, while the bad things fester and then seem to appear all at once? Cuddy didn't know.

And nor did it seem did anyone else.

Yet Cuddy saw it happen step by step, unable to stop it, unable to keep the future from overtaking the present. Hearing it before seeing it. Seeing it before living it. And through every new "usurpation", the servant devoured every scrap of printed treason he could lay his hands on. As Mister Paul subscribed to every newspaper and periodical known to the colonists, all delivered to the silver smithy ready to be passed around or read at once. And the Reading Negro, Cuddy, read them all, often in secret. For if the Crown's men raided the smithy and found some of those tracts, there'd be hell to pay. Expropriation. Arrest.

Worse perhaps … a disappearance, never to appear again. The woods and lakes were very big and not everyone who ventured out in the company of Redcoats came back again.

Cuddy often stashed a few of the broadsheets, periodicals and handbills in a corner of the belfry. A long way up, a long way down, who in their right mind would look for them there?

A few issues of The Royal American Magazine or American Monthly Museum, or Censor and countless handbills with engravings that showed Royal Officials, Members of Parliament, and British soldiers buggering helpless colonial maidens and gorging themselves on the carcass of one colonial silk stocking or another. But tonight, he didn't bother to light a candle or open them. Instead, he just cogitated…

A long, dark rumination. After all, he'd seen it for himself.

The storm between the Crown and their loyal colony had been building as long as he could recall, a decade at least. Back when those nasty Boston youngsters throwing horse dunged oyster shells at Redcoats hadn't even been born yet. Nor even those comely tavern maids spitting in the Lobsters' grog when the British fingers groped colonial petticoats.

Years past, fathers, mothers, aunts and uncles up and down the colonies were simply busy working the rhythm of life – all they wanted was to be left alone. But wars had drained the empire, and Mother Britain was desperate for funds. Wars won, wars lost, and wars still being fought. Some far from the shores of America, some next door. The colonies were simply too prosperous to ignore.

This raw land teamed with game, the coastal waters packed with fish, hills of endless timber, rivers and swamps of unlimited fur, valleys of bountiful grain and tobacco and corn and every crop worth a pence.

And another pence.

And another.

Like every generation, legions of factotums with pens at the ready stole from the living. Tax, tax, tax and tax some more. More to be squeezed, more to be milked. No man was so free that the dead hand of the Devil's quill would not seek to bind them, shackling them to the corpse of a bloated leprous state. The bleating sheep seeking mercy from a merciless administrative maw until they were slaughtered and consumed.

Like grit under your lip you could never spit out –

We make war in Europe, you pay.

We make war in Canada, you pay.

We make war in India, you pay.

Pay, pay, pay – then we'll war on you –

And still, you'll pay for that too.

Like every colonist, Cuddy's eyes threw daggers at the sight of a government official and the Royal Seal. The scowl of repressed rage. The Lion and Unicorn, two great beasts coming together to devour the world. The two animals, Lion and Unicorn, not noble creatures but carrion jackals.

And when posted on the side of a brick building, or a letterhead, or proclamation, it didn't even matter what the poster or proclamation proclaimed. Deface it. Burn it. Kill it. In place of the motto – *Dieu et Mon droit* – God and My right – scratch an X, rip the poster from the brick face, paint it over with an even more obscene word.

Royalist.

Or even better –

Sodomite.

Buggerer. Every scrawled X smiting the tyranny of legislators, those bespectacled root-chewing rodents. Underground vermin. Blind Moles. Furiously grinding away at the marrow of every enterprise.

Then emerging from their house of commons or house of lords as the grand panjandrums, expecting their prostrate colonies to thank them for the privilege of bending over and servicing their swollen members for a good old-fashioned ramming.

A pox on both their Houses – Lords and Commons – bleeding the New World white. One dastardly act of parliament after another, deserving no mercy, no quarter. One bill of attainder, printed commandment, glue specked poster pasted on every streetcorner, tavern door and shopfront. Cuddy watched them appear, furiously read, and ripped down. Thence back to England to be repealed – yet then sustained once again and reborn in Quasimodo form.

The Sugar Act.

All hail Lord Sugar, Master Molasses and the God King Rum. Once upon a time the Six Pence Tax per gallon on foreign molasses was simply never accounted for, never paid and in their infinite wisdom, their benevolent lordships reduced to Three Pence Tax – but this time Cuddy knew they meant it – no smuggling, no manufacture with Frenchie molasses, and thrown in for good measure a tax on wine, coffee – a necessity – and pimiento – a delicacy. Another tax on cambric so it cost more to make fine clothes, another tax on printed calico so it cost more to make pretty frocks. And regulate what you hadn't taxed – the export of iron, lumber, cheese, flour.

Cuddy watched every sailing brig and merchant ship, their hulls bursting at the seams, loaded down with all manner of hard goods. None of which goods stayed where they belonged – in colonial barn or home or hearth. Instead, the stocks, wares and commercial materiel went to the French West Indies, Madeira, the Azores and the Canary Islands, Santo Domingo, Martinique and Guadeloupe – all begging for iron, lumber, cheese and flour, farm products of any kind to make their islands livable. Turn around once and nothing a man harvested, or produced wasn't taxed, regulated, banned – then stolen by the Crown and shipped to another colony's slave and sugar plantations.

And Cuddy knew enough not to brush with the law under any circumstances. Look not for justice – look not to Boston or Philadelphia or Williamsburg or New York but – stand in the dock in faraway Canada. The Admiralty Court out of Halifax took up all matters from commerce in the colonies. Need Justice or a court of final jurisdiction? No local magistrate for you, bondsman.

Accused smuggler? Go to Canada or be hanged in Rhode Island. Or both – judged in Nova Scotia, then be shipped back across the ocean – hanged in the gallows, dancing the Tyburn jig.

The Crown corrupted everything it touched. Even money.

The Currency Act.

Cuddy thought it better named, The No Currency Act. Watching his fellow colonists damn the worthless paper money. Stupidity on Stilts. The paper money printed in the colonies, banned by the crown – but still allowed for public debts and taxes – just not private debts – a mishmash of can, can't, will, won't, with no other colonial recourse than to boycott the trade with the mother country. Without gold or sterling specie to back the paper, commerce turned to barter – Tobacco for script – and even then, you saved the best tobacco for export, the worst for exchange in debts public and private. So with Molasses, so with Rum so with…

The Stamp Act.

Cuddy found two scraps of paper in his pocket. Nearly rubbed to dissolution. A bit of rebellion he kept on his person. Once held by iron round his neck and ankles, Cuddy now understood how paper itself could hold a man just as fast.

Behold the stamp.

HONI SOIT QUI MAL Y PENSE

Shame on anyone who thinks evil of it.

And further down the chain of tyranny, a Death's Head – along its side, the brutal injunction printed for all to see:

> *The effects clear, the response immediate, inevitable death in every particular. O! the fatal Stamp:*
>
> *Where All Paper Used of any Kind Must Have an Embossed Stamp of Compliance and Imported from His Majesty. Bills, Posters, Letters, Certificates, Legal Instruments, Periodicals, Playing Cards… All on expensive, imported paper. And paid for in Pounds Sterling, not that Colonial whimsical script.*

You could feel primal rejection from Virginia to Maine. Cuddy along with every other colonial – puking up the imperial rule like an emetic administered by Francis Willis Royal Physician to His Majesty George III. Sir Doctor Quack.

The King is Always Right.

Even When His Majesty is Wrong.

Because the King is Always Right.

Until he's not.

Cuddy watched with growing fear as his fellows' rejection exploded to trade boycotts, and officials hung in effigy. And every poster of the Royal Seal with the Lion and the Unicorn torn from wall or defaced where they hung. Anger and defiance against the inviolate scales of Empire and the force of commerce. Taunting a reckoning.

The rejection of the Royal Edict was so forceful and so relentless, there was nothing left but abject surrender. Royal Retreat.

Enacted. Rejected. Repealed.

Yet His Majesty was too far away to reckon with. So, if you couldn't dethrone the King –

Then hang his legal representative. Make the King's Man, the hapless Governor Gage, the object of all derision. Abuse. And terror.

Cuddy balled up the damp rebel papers into a spitball and tossed them into a dark corner. No one would miss the governor. Good riddance.

He'd seen the reckoning with his own eyes.

Not so long ago, he stood in the street before the Governor's mansion when the rioters came. His master, Mr. Paul had sent him to deliver a finished silver gravy boat. And the black man held it in his hands as he turned the corner to the Governor's home. Hutchinson house, Garden Court Street, North End. Not far from the shop, nor the church he sat in now.

One of the finest houses in the province. Three stories bricked and chimneyed like a grand layer cake. Surrounded by a picket fence.

The mob swarmed the Governor's front steps like angry badgers. Smashed through the front door with an ax and rushed in, en masse. Hands and pry bars ripped the wainscoting from the mansion walls, tore down the hangings and chandeliers, and sconces, breaking every room in an orgy of rage.

Every picture stolen off its hook, every book, every paper, every manuscript. Every stick of furniture either carted away or broken into bits, every scrap of clothing in every closet shredded, featherbeds stabbed to death, feathers pouring out the windows. And £900 in ready sterling

Cuddy watched all night, frozen in place like a cigar store Indian, afraid to leave in case someone was harmed, afraid to lose the silver gravy boat, afraid to fetch his master in case he missed something even more wanton.

Dawn found the placed sacked with men upon the mansion roof, tearing the slate shingles free for other homes. Garden trampled to mud; fruit trees uprooted.

And so, Crown Troops came.

The Quartering Act.

Trespassers make a home in your garden, one rogue puts his muddy boots up on your kitchen table, another a boot on your neck. Didn't really matter that the Governor and Parliament forbade the quartering in private houses, the troops were everywhere. Locusts feeding on the fat of the land, except unlike locusts they didn't come from the skies but like garbage flies hovering over the stinking jetsam thrown from these massive, wooden hulks, floating in the harbor.

If the Colonials had named a Crown law regarding these ships, these floating garbage dumps, they might have called the Crown's oppressive presence The Petty Acts.

Returned in kind, the Colonials' own retribution – petty as well, but more than painful. Adding insult to injury:

Throwing oyster shells in snowballs, spitting in the tavern fare served to redcoats, slinging slop pails without looking, washerwomen losing clothes, boots fixed wrong with hobnail, poking the toes, laundresses scorching the fancy lace of officers and highborn ladies under the hot flat-iron, and then more troops.

In Boston alone, one newspaper cried:

We now behold the Representatives' Chamber Court-House, and Faneuil-Hall, those seats of Freedom and justice occupied with troops, and Guards placed at the doors; the Common covered With tents, and alive with soldiers; marching and Countermarching to relieve the guards, In short the town is now a perfect garrison.

The New York Restraining Act.

Another Colony in need of restraint.

Whereof the Assembly and Governor of New York shall pass no law until colony of New York fully complies with the Quartering Act.

Hereafter pay for all housing, food and supplies of the Redcoats garrisoned there. Pay up or die, New York.

The Revenue Act.

Glass, lead, painters' colors, paper – tax it. Smugglers subject to writs of assistance, open warrants allowing customs officials to search any dwelling, seize any goods. Not so the British subject. In Britain your private property was private. Here in the Colonies, your private property was owned by the Crown's mercenaries and men at arms.

The Indemnity Act.

A charmed cobra snake dance of protection for the East India Company's tea. A Gargantua of commerce and importation – everyone knew the massive enterprise of the East India Company was now on the verge of financial collapse. Yes, the colonies could get their tea cheaper from the Dutch – and NO – they weren't allowed to buy from anyone but England.

Now we go after the smugglers –

The Commissioners of Customs Act. A new board of customs commissioners to be headquartered in Boston. Another bureaucracy, another chance to tax and round up smugglers. Blue-nosed customs commissioners backed up by armed troops. As for the smugglers… Cuddy knew their fate: Catch 'em, try 'em, hang 'em.

The Vice Admiralty Court Act.

Another hangman for the smugglers, not the colonial courts but the Royal Naval courts – three new admiralty courts in Boston – craven, lickspittle Judges appointed by the Crown. And adding insult to injury, the Crown awarded their judges a 5% slice of any fine levied. Making it pay handsomely to fine, pay handsomely to levy, pay handsomely to adjudicate. And the appointed judge was the sole arbiter of truth, no trial by Jury. All appearances before the court to be made in Boston and if the smuggler failed to appear, an automatic verdict of guilty. Wagon broke on the road, horse dies in harness, drops dead in a downpour, no traffic either way – miss your court date?

Guilty. Guilty. Guilty.

Pay your fine.

Fail to pay.

Wear the iron shackles of a prison barge.

That cold embrace Cuddy knew all too well.

Back in the belfry, Cuddy looked out over the bay; the gargantuan hulks of the warships floated on the water, like a motionless menace. A sailor on one of the ships marched aft holding a lantern, a small dot of light on the black beast. The light vanished as the seaman descended into the hold.

Faintly Cuddy heard the chime of the ship's bells, marking the change of watch. Two plus two plus two. Six Bells. Eleven o'clock. Then all the other ships chimed in. Not all the midshipmen or masters-at-arms kept the same timepiece. Or kept the same time, always a few moments off. The noise of the bells rang faintly then faded across the water. The chimes lingered for a moment in the belfry and then went to God. Silence returned.

How had it come to this? Ships in the bay with gunners and gunners' mates and powder boys swabbing their cannon? With musket-toting soldiers onshore in every street, poking a bayonet up every skirt to get a peek? Every magistrate and solicitor a wormy English turnip bubbling in your bowels? How?

Act after Act after Act.

The Tea Act tore a huge hole in trust. A trick tax because otherwise the Crown couldn't get its grip about the throat of commerce. Because it couldn't be done any other way besides illegitimate underhanded billing.

Cuddy took a long swallow from his bottle of tea. Cuddy knew nothing of tea when he first arrived, but over time he learned. Along with reading and writing and arithmetic. Mr. Revere the elder had made sure of that. And all the fuss they made over this simple drink ebbed and flowed with each new regulation. Until no one wanted to drink it any longer.

They called the tea, Bohea. The import. A dark draught of black and oolong that could keep you alert for a fortnight. The Chinese cultivated it, then baled it, then brought it on their backs to ports of call. How much massive energy and effort went into sending it around the world? And how much profit? Cuddy didn't know. But he knew the price men paid. Money enough to grow empires or crush nations.

If men could make property of men, they could make property of anything.

Cuddy knew that all too well. Expropriate in the name of fairness, honesty, integrity – and bestow it to anyone but the rightful owner, dead or alive. Slavery was still an honest trade across the seven seas. And commerce what men made of it – whether it be a cask of iron nails or a man in an iron collar. Slavery poisoned honest commerce, transforming it into a cunning, evil, ravenous creature. Turning ownership – into a ha'penny trollop to be ravaged by the score, used up, and left in the gutter like horse dung in the street.

The Whore of Babylon seducing all men to her dry, barren bosom.

Cuddy knew about desperation.

He'd seen it a lifetime ago in a Barracoon when slavers turned him into a slave. He'd seen it in the bowels of a slaver bark. And he saw it every moment of his life as men turned on other men for their own advantage. Cuddy may not have known every detail in the great game of commerce, but he knew the human animal.

And if the great East India Tea Company was on the verge of bankruptcy, whose fault was that beside Parliament? All the Tea in China sat in their British warehouses as British taxes made the tea too expensive to sell in Bristol or the world. Yet East India, a company immune, exempt from failure – would sell it where they could.

Sell it to the Colonies, cheaper than the Dutch smuggled tea. Leave off an import tax going into Britain, pick up three pence on the other side of the Atlantic where the Colonials couldn't complain, besides – by law – the rustics couldn't buy tea from any other source than the Crown. Captive buyers.

And more besides, the Colonists' Import companies of Richard Clarke and the sons of Governor Thomas Hutchinson of Massachusetts bought direct. Massachusetts Merchants thriving off the Crown, men connected, important men and families earning filthy lucre at the expense of their underlings.

No good would come of this.

Stop! Don't! Wait!

Sage counsels on both sides of the ocean cried. But to no avail. Dire warnings, all ignored. The Special Men at home – profiteers – the Special Men in parliament employing thumb-screws. Honorable Statesmen.

Jackass Lord North wanted that three pence to pay his colonial lackeys. Officials at every level of colonial governance, bought and paid for by the Crown. The King's Men, not the Colonies'.

Buy the Tea we send you. Buy it and shut up. Buy it because that's what we tell you. Buy it and like it.

And if you don't want it, take it anyway, stuff your bed pillows and cushions with it. Feed it to your horses and cattle.

Cuddy watched from Mr. Paul's shops as ships arriving at the colonies' ports were turned away. Refused harbor. Too late for compromise. Too late for anything but anger.

Piss in Redcoat's cocked hat, piss in your precious tea.

Piss on the Crown's Men of Consignment. Everywhere you turned in the streets of Boston livid wall posts shouted from every wall, door and even shop windows:

To the TEA CONSIGNEES – you are odious miscreant and detestable Tools Traitors to your Country," even going so far as to call such men "Butchers". In a ploy to strike such dread as to make the Crown's lackeys resign out of fear for their very lives. Chief harasser, an angry fellow anonymously named "JOYCE, jun" Joyce Junior. The mysterious: (Chairman of the Committee for Tarring and Feathering.

The anger built. And Cuddy could do nothing about it. The simmering, bitter froth washed over the bays and riverbanks like an incoming tide. Especially in Massachusetts where the Governor's sons ran their own import business and defying the rabble, demanded to know why in Heaven's name shouldn't they bring those crates of cheap tea into their warehouses. Sell it in Boston, sell it up and down the seaboard. No dammit, the Gub and his sons wouldn't let the ships sail back to England full.

Full ships waiting to disgorge their tea, full ships embargoed but still in port.

Cuddy watched as the crowd of wrath at Faneuil Hall shouted for deportation. A thousand souls inside, more thousands gathered in the square. But unruly mobs by nature do unruly things and this crowd left the hall to cheer more rebel theatrics from the dockside. Political histrionics, and more the dangerous for it.

A hundred torches lit the wharfs about the bay. From Griffin's Wharf the raiders sculled across the water, not silently but to the hoarse cheers of the crowd. People kept surging to the docks' end, some almost falling in, then grabbed by others before they went over the edge.

A dozen boats with oarsmen, glided toward the three cargo ships anchored in harbor. The oarsman dressed in deerskins and Mohawk feathers – Injun Raiding Party – the message clear – these raiders were on the side of the shore-bound wrathful crowd, up and down the riverbank, the Colonists, the Natives. Not the bewigged fart-catchers sitting on their benches in the House of Parliament, not the King on his throne, not the Crown's men cowering in their fine Boston homes. Not the angry red lobsters patrolling every street and road.

The noise from the ships drifted across the bay, their bright feathered war bonnets flashed in the light of lantern and torch. The sounds of men stomping up and down into the ships' holds, the grunts and shouts as crates were hefted upwards, the crack-crack of hatchets' splitting the crates, exposing the fragrant wads of baled tea crammed within. Some poured out till empty, others just tossed overboard with a few holes to sink them.

Splash after splash as each crate went into the drink. Crate after crate after crate, almost too many to count. More than three hundred – enough tea to satisfy, to quench the thirst of Massachusetts for a year. And Cuddy wondered how long it would be before he drank another cup of oolong. Long time, he thought…

The torches waved along the shoreline of the bay, cheers from bank to ship and back again.

Cuddy remained on the wharf side till every crate went into the water, till every crate sank or bumped up against shore. The grunts of men, the splash in the drink, the silent ripples of every evil crate. Then back to the shop. Once again, Mr. Paul had sent him to deliver finished silver to the Governor. This time a sugar bowl. Cuddy rode out of town on a young mule named Mabel but found the Governor not at home.

Rather Cuddy found the man standing with his wife, children and servants in a high field overlooking the town. Like some witnesses at prayer meeting, standing as a group all staring in the same direction. Back down at Boston. Down below the celebrations were still in full swing. The harbor, aglow with torches and the sound of distant bells chiming hosannas to the ruin.

From the dark hill the Governor, his family, his servants watched the madness running roughshod over all and sundry, the madness of men in revolt breaking bit and harness. Knowing once and for all, there was nothing a Governor, any governor, could do.

The lordly man took the sugar bowl in its paper wrapping from Cuddy's hands. Turning it over, he examined it carefully. Plain and unadorned, a squat goblet with a domed lid, fit tight as a drum. Even in the night, silver had a luster that glittered in your eyes. Polished and smooth, without frills or filigree – how much like the people down below. These "Colonists". The rabble, the hardy folk of Boston Bay, the flinty New Englander face thickened by tough winters, hands chapped, and milkmaids with cheeks red as apples in Fall. The Governor was going to miss this place.

He handed the sugar bowl to a servant who wrapped it in another cloth and clutched it to his breast. They tore their eyes from the fire in the bay and to the lanterns on the road.

The coach was ready.

By dawn broken crates washed along the wharves, their contents strewn out like the entrails of a gutted bladder, other crates rocking against breakwater boulders amongst the broken oyster shells and bay trash.

But that night, Cuddy saw Governor Hutchinson mount his coach. And in so doing, the governor bid farewell to America. His coach and horses taking him first to Canada and then away for good.

Crown's Governor Hutchinson gone to England. Never to see Boston again.

Chapter Seven: Intolerable

Steeple, Old North Church
Midnight

Over the course of a lifetime Cuddy had seen it all for himself. Their ugly situation growing knotted, tangled and twisted, worse by month and year. A cold resolved seemed to have descended on the colony, on the city proper. An endless winter of resentment. Colder than the drafty belfry.

Governor fled.

Crown's Assets plundered.

Property destroyed.

Scrofulous Royal Tea rejected; cold coffee drunk by the gallon now. Hot or cold Java from the blue mountains of Jamaica – Black Tom some called it – suddenly the colonist's swill of choice. A slave-labor drink. Beans grown by the bushel under whip and chain. Begging the question – could anyone, a free soul or indentured serf, drink anything made without the cheap sweat of a bond slave?

But it wasn't slave labor the Crown objected to, but rebellion against its God-given right to hold sway.

This is what could not stand. Their right to rule.

The Crown would have the final say in the affairs of their possessions, to determine once and for all who was master, who laid down law and who obeyed.

Matters required coercion. Force of law and action.

And when matters require such coercion, matters soon become intolerable.

First, His Majesty demanded restitution for goods destroyed – those damn dumped and broken crates – 342 odd chests, 92,000 lbs, 46 tons – enough tea to warm the cockles of Boston proper, the entire Massachusetts colony and greater New England for a year! Estimated value: £9659. A fortune, with every man, woman and merchant, every member of Boston common on the hook for the damages.

Object to the culpability and burden?

Desire redress?

Not in this lifetime, colonial mollusk. Go to hell, peasant.

Eat Crown dung.

No redress on State Street. No redress in Providence, no redress in Richmond or New York. In the Bay area, the Massachusetts Charter was eliminated by Parliament, and every man jack, every pego, and mantrap of local government replaced by the King's Buggers and Toadies. No meetings but once a year. Obey.

And if any royal official might overstep his powers, there'd be no trial within the Colonies, instead, maybe a hearing in Halifax, maybe sailed back to clammy Britain, safe from certain American Justice.

Better to play everyone off against the other. When there are two sides to every tale, you'll find a dozen sides. All competing for prominence. Better to sow confusion, ignore evidence. Ignore witnesses. Better to seize the levers and grinding gears of the law to the Crown's ends, leaving the devil to the hindmost.

Yet there was much sport to be had. The profitable business of selling spirits, beer, whiskey, rum to Redcoats. And the delightful game of getting Redcoats to puke their uniforms and piss themselves as they staggered about Boston Town in search of their cot. A trooper could stone himself to oblivion on a copper. And two coppers guaranteed a stupefaction that lasted well into their next day's duty. Many a soldier came down with a case of the Staggers. And staggering men could be seen at all hours clinging to building fronts and supporting themselves on iron hitching posts.

Each and every drunkard a mark for the cunning lads with slingshots. Enterprising young fellows out after bedtime. The urchins watched every tavern door for the Staggers. Taking aim, letting fly a stone then ducking for cover before the drunkard could turn around. A good hit on the ear or neck knocked a man to the ground. Nicknamed, a "Knickerbocker". And the little bastards now called Liberty Boys striking a blow against the Crown with every stinger.

Cuddy had seen the Slingers often enough at night, as he passed to and from his patron's smithy and Mr. Paul's house. And more often than not, Cuddy had words for the young truants, scolding the louts back into the shadows from which they came. For every stone slung, another Redcoat would despise Boston. For every stone that found a soft spot on a Redcoat neck came a wound and outrage that would never heal. For every Knickerbocker came a moment of vengeance just waiting for release and the right moment of reckoning.

How had it come to this? One Knickerbocker at a time. And no good came of it. Worse still, the Redcoats were under orders not to retaliate, beat or horsewhip the colonists. Instead, they vented their rage on any creature that couldn't testify. Cuddy saw them doing the most unspeakable things to animals. Catching rats in burlap sacks, then throwing them in a fire. Cutting cat's tails. Kicking dogs or slamming them with the butts of guns when no one was looking. Anything to relieve the pressure.

High up in the church tower, Cuddy lit the candle, dripped some wax and planted it on the wooden floor. You couldn't change the past. He clutched a nappy blanket around him. A fine spring night but still damp. The moist bay air filled the belfry and clung to every surface. A cold roost till tomorrow's sunrise.

Down below he listened for the soldiers. Every night brought the Staggers singing hoarsely on the happy upswing of their swigging, but tonight nothing. Boston was quiet, empty of Redcoats. They'd all gotten in their boats and paid the Ferryman to cross the river. Every man at arms across the Charles by now, the officers mustering their forces. Soon they would head inland.

Anchored on the dark water, the huge hulk of the HMS Somerset flashed glints of silver and brass where the moon tricked out her fittings. The small boats of the river ferry tied up alongside, like wolf pups at a mama's teat. After nine o'clock no river traffic was allowed. No passage either way. British command locked the city down and cut off Charleston.

From his chilly perch in the church tower, Cuddy could see the black bay, but not the skiff. Yet the mind is a powerful force, the human imagination even more so. Easy to imagine the water under his master's keel.

The skiff's oars dipped quietly and slowly; the oarlocks padded so as not to make the slightest clink. The blade dipped in, the oar pulled out. A master rower could row his boat as quietly as required. Indeed, a skiff on a waterway was many things, a herald, a spy, an army in the fog, a ghost passing in the night. Again, the two watermen dipped the oars and let them drip free, then dip again. No sailor or officer in the great HMS Somerset any the wiser…

Mr. Paul had been lucky with more than just the tide sweeping him across.

The moon his friend too. Tonight, it rose deep in the Southeast, and not before half past nine. The moon slowly climbed over the town, silhouetting the rooftops and belfry. The great ship's lookouts stared into that bright face, yet the water of the bay remained black as sin. Leaving Mr. Paul and his rowers unnoticed as they skulled silently across to safety and waiting horsemen.

Before long the skiff reached a narrow floating dock. Not quite a pier, but a wood-plank landing, just sturdy enough to keep your feet dry, just buoyant enough to bounce when a watercraft tied alongside. It dipped as Mr. Paul abandoned the boat, then sank a little under his weight.

Two men on horseback waited on the bank. The Colonel and the Deacon. Both men's faces cloaked and partially hidden, dark, stiff figures like cemetery sculptures.

In his mind, Cuddy could hear his master address the two statues.

"Come, come now," Mr. Paul would softly say. "Bad as all that?"

One of the men, sour as a pickle, "Did you remember your spurs this time? So you can ride with some alacrity?"

"Aye." Mr. Paul showed his spurs, gleaming dully in his fist. "Not at first. So I told m'dog to run home and fetch m'spurs. Wear 'em later. Had to send him home with a note, but he plum f'got wadding for the oars."

A long and doubtful silence from the two cold pickles on horseback. Dogs fetching spurs, a tavern tale. "You got yer wadding though."

As if to prove Mr. Paul's point, one of the oarsmen plucked what looked like half a white nightie from one oarlock and then the other. The two torn pieces of nightgown seemed to fit together. The rowers' oar wadding, rendering their sculling mute as a pillar.

"Still warm when it fell from the bedroom window."

"Anyone we know?"

"A gentleman never tells, Deacon. But you can be assured she didn't need it as she was quartering a Lieutenant Major in the 5th. At the time, not at home. No doubt on the march inland this night."

The Deacon piously crossed himself. "Our women know no end of sacrifice."

Cuddy knew the lady in question, of course. The Spinster Markham, chaste as a church mouse; owner of any number of housecoats and nightgowns. Now, at least they'd pressed the spinster's garment into the service of a patriot.

Besides Mr. Paul's stern riders, others across the river in Charleston would have seen the two lamps in Christ Church tower. And known immediately what it meant and what was to be done when the British left their barracks to march the night –

Ride cross country, secure Rebel ordinance. Keep all and sundry moving their goods from pillar to post, hiding it hither and yon. A few days ago, Mr. Paul went across the river on a looksee, up and down the Medford Road getting those in Concord to move the stash of guns, powder, shot and supplies. If the local Yankees hadn't by now, they'd better hide it soon.

Then – finally – if anyone remembered – alert the leaders of the rebellion, if any could be found.

Plenty of worthies hiding in the countryside, if anyone bothered to look. Easy enough for them to move around, hide in a cottage, a barn or in a moonlit field.

The most notable –

Paunch Adams, that talking turnip man, John Adams. And the other "John" – Pinch Hancock that hatchet-nosed, thin-lipped dandy.

Cuddy took the thought back, too harsh the criticism by far. He'd only met those two worthies once, and only in passing at Mr. Paul's shop. Cuddy was always careful of a poor man's envy. Envy didn't increase your own wealth but left unchecked could poison the soul as your fortune grew. And if not firmly locked in the broom closet of one's mind – envy became a cripple's crutch – envy for all, sympathy for none

Besides…

Freedom had been good to Mister Cuddy. Mr. Paul good to him as well. Boston good to him. All good to him. A far better world than slavery or Africa.

Waiting in the church belfry was more than a perch, less than a refuge – a drafty redoubt of sight and promise. Anticipation and fear. Knowing he could see the future of the night ahead, like a map laid out on a table, showing every man's actions and every man's thoughts. But never knowing if his own thoughts and prayers for those across the countryside would be heard by the Almighty, and if heard – be answered.

In his own human way Cuddy knew many across the river felt exactly the same. Filled with a stern and righteous anger, knowing the years of exploitation and abuse had reached their limits. That a call to arms was only that, a call, a bugle across the field. A beaten drum drawing all who heard it to the sound. That if there was to be a war, a battle or strife, everlasting men need hear that call, hear the bugle, hear the drum, and if not tomorrow – tonight.

People, knowing in their hearts, they must leave home and hearth this dark night – if what they had carved out of rocky Massachusetts was not to be crushed to dust and oyster shells. No, go out, hear the call, listen for the bugle, run to the drum. For the time come for every patriot to secure the Almighty's benevolence in this night's work. Rebel goods and rebel worthies – keep them safe at all costs – safe and hidden for the day they were needed.

So, Cuddy could see across the river, see as well and hear as well as if he'd been standing there himself…

On the far bank near the rocking dock, Mr. Paul and his two stern horsemen saddled Rose, a fine animal and willing to ride at any time of day or night. And most thankfully, totally ignorant of Redcoats, the Crown, Tea, Acts, and reports of Regulars on the march.

Cuddy wished he could be with them, especially riding with Mr. Paul – but his old bones didn't sit a horse as they used to. More often, a mule. While an old man's midnight time, though often wakeful was little stronger in body than when he laid himself down for bed. And as Cuddy lay his stiff shanks down upon the pew cushion, the belfry beams stared down at him, like a many-pointed star. He tried to count them but kept counting the same one twice and wearily gave up.

His eyes grew too heavy, fluttering slits, while in his mind, he heard or thought he heard hoofbeats, hoofbeats galloping into the night, and bells, bells from every spire along the road, ringing under the moon, into the night.

While underneath it all – the constant padding of a drum.

Chapter Eight: Midnight March

April 19th, 2:00 AM.
The Lexington Road

Belle was a good, even-tempered mare. Smooth, steady. Lieutenant Moreau chose not to ride her, but lead his mount, the dependable, sweet Belle by the halter. So even if the soldiers made fun of their officer without a stallion for a mount –

His men always knew three things about Moreau's command.

First, he always spared the mare when he could.

Second, he spared the men as well. For the Lieutenant never rode when the men marched, but marched alongside them, to and from battle. Thereby sparing the horse for actual combat. And his men the envy of watching him astride a mount.

And thirdly, that the sweet and patient Belle was often used for the wounded, if such could ride, sent back to camp or barracks ahead of any advance or retreat. Thereafter, Moreau would fight on foot.

The men had even seen Moreau do the unthinkable. He allowed the good Belle to work in service of the locals. Once on patrol, they came upon a woman pulling a hand-cart, struggling with all her might. A damsel-in-distress. The Lieutenant dismounted, saying quietly, "Here now, young woman. This is no work for you." Gently hitching his mare up to the handcart and letting the woman walk alongside unburdened. The officer asking politely, "May I know your name?"

The lady looked at him with amazed eyes. As if never encountering such a gentleman before on a rude country road such as this. "Mary. Of the Hartwell Tavern. Next time you're there, I'll stand you drinks." And the Moreau nodded without a word.

Such manner of command had the effect pacifying the locals and of binding his men together. Leaving the colonial resentments and the constant grumbling of the King's soldiers in their proper place. With any luck, a mile or so behind the marching column in the hanging dust.

Sure, there might have been musket or powder in the woman's cart, but not the motherload. And spreading a little goodwill cost less, even if you let slip your military intentions. Resentment always cost more. And there are worse things than looking the fool.

Yet who sees dust at night? You can taste the marching dust, and feel the veneer of it on your face, and crusts in the corners of your eyes. You could brush it away between cadence, or wipe it off with a damp cloth, but in the end, you felt its dry caress on every bit of exposed skin and every bit of dangling weaponry. The sword grip, the musket, your canteen.

No man spoke, breathing easy as they strode along. Lieutenant Moreau walked apart. Muddled memories seemed to crawl into his mind from his boots upwards. A week past he'd attended a concert at Faneuil Hall, packed to the rafters with rowdy redcoats and loyalists come to see any bit of entertainment. The Nightingale. The single stage show allowed in this dank colony.

The singer, *une femme d'un certain âge* and then some, must have been pretty back when she sang on the Edinburgh stage for hairy Scotsmen. But a decade's time had not been kind. The life of a stage singer turned the charming songbird into a molting harridan. Still, the audience gave her three encores and a basket of sifted flour baked bread instead of flowers. Any show in a storm so to speak.

But worse was yet to come.

Only a few hours later, Lieutenant Moreau found himself waking in a creaking bed by the singer's side. So much for Meg in Mayfair. The vague recollection of meeting Lola Feathers in the tavern, which tavern? He didn't remember. Long smiles and silly nothings, as drinks came and went – then a stumble up a narrow bit of stairs, a horrid bit of rutting and finally snores. Eyes open to that blinding hangover of the doomed, Moreau stared into her sagging face. She drooled on her pillow as she slept and Moreau found his own face sticky to the touch.

Yet even as he marched, an even worse recollection came down from on high, or perhaps, up from below … less personal failure than regimental failure. A young soldier, Corporal McNaught of the King's Own was put on trial for abuse of a local fisherman. Seems the fishy fishmonger wouldn't sell his cod, but when plied with coin relented selling the soldier a gutted flap of fish flesh. Only to spit on the gutted thing as he wrapped it in a dirty rag. Corporal McNaught tossed the length of fish back at the cur none too gently, then demanded return of his coin.

The fisherman refused, claiming once sold, there could be no return. More argument ensued, and a struggle where Corporal McNaught wrested his few coins back by plucking the fishmonger's purse from greasy coat pockets, in a bit of street corner angling.

Hence the charge of assault, a Court of Enquiry, a search for witnesses testifying to less than nothing. And Corporal McNaught placed under arrest and confined to regimental quarters. Namely the blockhouse.

In the name of the King, the Commanding officer of the Regiment sent word to McNaught in the blockhouse that if the soldier apologized to the fishmonger all charges would be dropped and the Corporal could return to duty. McNaught refused unless ordered in writing to apologize and requested instead a General Court Martial.

All over a few coins and a stinking slab of cod.

In the end the Commanding Officer released his Corporal without prejudice. And Corporal McNaught went on to cement his reputation for hasty, impulsive action by walking from the blockhouse that very night and consuming so much Yankee Rum that he pitched headfirst over a seawall and cracked his skull on the rocks below. The morning change of guard found the Corporal half floating, face down in the tide.

This whole business fairly skewered it for Lieutenant Moreau. The inhabitants of this vile city didn't want them there. And wouldn't have cared if every Redcoat in Boston caught the pox as long as no one swilled from the same cup. Every soldier in the colony despised every filthy bugger they passed in the street. His men had swallowed more spit, endured more taunts, and suffered every bruise flung from some little beggar's slingshot. A wonder the men didn't snatch the first boy they found walking alone by himself and bugger the lad in the nearest alley just for the fun of it.

Oh, the Crown loved their Massachusetts colony dearly. And not one Redcoat was slated to cut the Knott of his service until Parliament, the Lords and King squeezed every penny they could from this damp, cold place.

Lieutenant Moreau shifted his unslung saber over his shoulder and glanced heavily at the sky. Dark trees passed on either side, but in the swath of open sky that same moon, silver, white and fanciful smiled down as if she didn't have a care in the world.

In the black moon-shadow of a gorse bush, the Lieutenant came upon Corporal Cummins sitting on his bum getting loose a boot. He'd struggled it to the point of messing with his buttoned gaiters, neither on nor off. The corporal looked up sharply as Moreau strode past.

"Got a stone in the mud somehow. Stone in the mud."

How the corporal got a pebble in his boot crawling barefoot off the mud bank was anyone's guess, but Lieutenant Moreau didn't dispute the crisis.

"Well, hurry up, Cummins. Let's not turn insufferable pebbles into a Shakespearean tragedy."

A quizzical look crossed the corporal's face, but he kept on fussing.

The night sky overhead was fine, a slight breeze in the tree-tops, the rustle of leaves. A rising moon shone down hard, making shadows of soldiers' forms. Lieutenant Moreau let his men break ranks and walk easy. A back-country march like this was no place for a noisy close order drill as Sergeant Bates ordered on the parade ground. A forced march on this pleasant night as sweet as any lovers' stroll, the trees in leaf passing on either side, a wisp of cloud across the moon's white face, so much better than the barracks, the dank taverns, the crushed oyster shell-lined streets of Boston with a Knickerbocker lurking behind ever wall.

Still, as they passed house or farm or hamlet, the men saw and heard the alarms spreading far and wide. Cat calls at their passing and the report of firearms. The clang of triangles hung from porch beams, and the warning smoke of cook fires wafting into the air, anything that would carry a message.

Suddenly, Moreau heard footsteps up ahead. The rushed footfalls of a man in a hurry. The steps grew closer, then loud and banging. In a moment the man appeared, soldier from one of the advance companies. Striding, trotting back along the line. He'd abandoned his cloak, his firearms, his haversack and was nearly running. A man in a rush with fear clinging to him like a cloying smell.

"What now, Soldier?" the Lieutenant called out.

Without breaking stride or slowing down the man hurried on, panting out his answer:

"No contact. No resistance yet, but command doesn't like it. They're calling for reinforcements. Additional men!" And then in another ten strides the trooper vanished down the road into the dark.

And in a flash of deep military insight, Lieutenant Moreau realized, that no matter when the trooper arrived at the Charles River or regimental command – the requested troops would be too late. Too late for the morning's rumble when and if – it occurred.

An uneasy quiet returned to his marching column. No one likes seeing soldiers fleeing in the wrong direction. A dark omen that only men advancing to the front would understand. Anyone, anyone moving, retreating, backing off along the line put a kind of doubt into every man jack of them.

A man running the wrong way, a black auger – like the chill you feel sitting on a headstone. Cold headstones, even in the summer.

Cold sweat and fear.

Chapter Nine: Alarmums

April 19th, 9:00 PM Onwards.
Various Farms, Taverns and Rustic Locations. A Nighttime Ride.

Riding hard, down a road, across a field, then galloping back on the road again. Irresistible, charging forward – man and animal fused into a single hurtling force. Pounding hooves driving the thoughts from your skull. The horse's hide lathered in sweat, your thighs gripping invincible girth. While the mount knew only the spur and the urgency, the crop and your will. Flying onward into the night, his gallop your gallop, a single creature gasping for air.

Earlier, two Royal Lobsters had nearly caught Mr. Paul and his mare Rose on the Medford Road. Riders burst out of the darkness – the King's interlopers cut off horseman and horse. But in the tricky dark, a clay pond appeared out of nowhere in an otherwise gentle field and swallowed one royal rider, sucking him into the muck. While Rose, a better horse by far, lost the other pursuer with a few digs of the heel. A better horse beat a lesser horse, and Mr. Paul left both stalkers in the rough.

Free of the Redcoats, good Rose cantered hard. House after house. The silversmith relayed the warning. "Alarum and Muster" – clattering into a farmyard in the dead of night, the dwelling lights doused, and curtains yanked aside. Mr. Paul felt more house burglar than parade ground drummer. Then hearing his nickname, from every watchful homeowner –

"Right, Mr. Paul," and "Thank you, Mr. Paul," his name issuing from every muffled lip. How odd that the African shop steward had been the first to call him that. And somehow Mr. Cuddy's moniker, Mr. Paul had caught on across the province; just like The Rogue's March, sung to the tune of that silly song, Poor Old Tory, used and abused by every side in this conflict:

Gave me a gun and a big red coat

Gave me lots of drilling

If I knew then what I know now

I wouldn't have took the shilling

The damn tune had forced itself into Mr. Paul's head, going round and round, mangling the lyrics into something even more absurd:

Poor old Paul, poor old Paul

Took him a horse to ride against vandals

If he knew what he knew now

He wouldn't have lit the belfry candles

And for every homestead warned, another rider sprang to life and galloped off. As if on Hermes' winged sandals, the fabled talaria – the heralds of rebellion spread the word. Pots and pans banged, bells rang, trumpets blew, firearms discharged – a cacophony of noise, notifying anyone within earshot – telling them, "Get ready, dammit!"

Now, after nearly being chased down and caught, Mr. Paul muttered the damn song to himself with every mile of ridden road. Hammering the stupid lyrics into his brain over every nighttime stride that he literally had to stop his mouth before hammering on a door and crying out, It's Me, poor old Paul, it's Me, Mr. Paul!

Instead, with the barest presence of mind, ride up to house or cottage, hissing in a harsh whisper to a dark door or shuttered window, "Get Ready! They're coming!"

At which point the door or window creaked open and a hushed voice hissed back, "Oh it's you, Mr. Paul!" Then spur away to the next cottage, the next lodging, the next farm. Leaving only a swirl of dust in the yard and an echo in the trees.

The problem wasn't so much going house to house but avoiding the patrols. You never knew where a squad of Lobsters would appear. Regimental commands were sending soldiers out at all times in small groups or even singly on horseback. Redcoats were always about, even before the main mass tramped West from Charleston. A few strings of hungry uniformed men scouring the countryside to count the chickens in every yard. And whatever else they could steal.

Here, there, everywhere. Popping up out of thin air then vanishing into the brush, almost as soon as they appeared. Off to God knows where.

Go down any length of road, any village green, clusters of armed onlookers milled about. A fine night, no reason to stay indoors. Chatting with friend or neighbor, sitting under a tree or on any low stone wall, word spread fast, far and wide.

Along the Bay Road in Lincoln, the Hartwell Tavern was open for business as usual. After 9 o'clock Mary Hartwell still worked her books of account.

Bleary-eyed, the proprietor's leather-bound account ledger seemed to hover before her face. Mary rubbed her eyes, the bitter dregs of cold coffee in a dented tin cup made no appeal. But her eyes glazed over and the sounds from her smoky den and softer noises from outside swathed her head in cobwebs. Horses' hoofs fading down the road and into the night.

Where was Sukey?

Oh yes, Sukey, their Negress – had gone outside again to gather wood chips from around the chopping block. Woodchip kindling for tomorrow's fires. Nothing worse than waking up on a damp morning and finding no dry wood, no dry kindling and dew covering everything that might burn. At that moment, the tavern door flung open and her servant stood there, spilling chips from her apron.

"Oh, Mistress Hartwell, there's a funeral going by!" Sukey blurted out.

Nowk

At nine o'clock? In the dark of night?

The tavern-keep put down her quill, capped the inkpot and closed the ledger. At the tavern door Mary Hartwell saw what Sukey saw.

Riders clopping by in single file.

Riders in the night.

The moon overhead made the road a silver path. The tavern-keep counted nine shadowed horsemen. British Redcoats black-booted and disguised in dark blue cloaks to hide their lobster backs, so they blended into the night. Slowly the soldiers passed before the Hartwell Tavern like risen figures on Judgement Day.

But Mary Hartwell knew better.

A small squad of cavalry. The soldiers probably dined near Boston at Cambridge only a few hours before. Then ordered out by Regimental Command to patrol west up the Old Bay Road. A troop in search of supplies or notable Provincials. Local men and Bostonians on the list, not your average Pompkins. A dark horseman's cloak suddenly flapped open and the glint of steel flashed under the moon. Matchlock pistol on one side, saber grip on the other.

The soldier clutched the flapping cloak, closed again. The glint vanished. But not the flash of his eyes. And Mary Hartwell didn't like the way the Lobster looked at her. Even in the dark, she felt the veiled threat, we know all about you, Tabby. You and all your toss pots. Your stink hole and your black-faced fart-catcher. You're on our list.

An angry, twisted stare. The soldier's face like a rictus mask on Halloween. Resentment, hate and choler. This man just waiting for an excuse to inflict some pain. Not at all like that brief encounter with that sad Lieutenant. Not at all like the kind officer who lent her a horse to pull her hand-cart. The briefest of respites.

A tender moment.

Here today, and gone tomorrow. Now long past. Fading into dim memory.

Mary Hartwell dropped her eyes in fear and a stab of shame.

She owed this redcoat thug no respect, but it was the pistol and sabers he carried she respected. And what a trained Lobster could do with such weapons in the art of war.

These riders might be going far as Concord, another ten miles. Everyone knew about the rebels' stores of arms and ammunition. The whole thing had become a shell game on a street corner, finding the cup and balls. Their minute men spent more time moving material and supplies from place to place than scrounging for more. The locals more afraid to lose what they already possessed. A lucky haul of powder and ball off the back of a field piece caisson would bring down the wrath of General Gage for sure. Hell, maybe it all boiled down to – grab what you can when you can. Gage was coming anyway.

The Redcoats had yet another reason to keep watch on the roads. Always on the lookout for any rolling conveyance, hand-cart or mule-drawn farm wagon. The cargo bin holding a few muskets under a blanket or canvas bags full of lead ball or powder horns.

An occupied, patrolled road was the King's Road. The Lobsters knew that as long as they patrolled, no messenger from Boston could reach Concord with news of a large British expedition. The King's soldiers knew full well this is what the locals feared most – a massive, invincible contingent on a deep foray into the countryside for hidden military stores and Provincial leaders. So, you salt the roads with soldiers, pick up rebel riders from Charleston and Boston. Do a thorough looksee. Then send in Gargantua, a red-coated giant.

The horsemen clicked their spurs and the horses cantered out of sight.

Back in the tavern, smoke hung in the air, thicker than before. Could Mary escape for a moment and tell their folk? Send word of the soldiers' approach? Someone had to get the word out about the patrol. Captain Smith of the Lincoln Minute Men didn't live too far. Mary Hartwell made a count of customers to see if she could sneak away. The more people drinking and getting stupid the better. Mary might not be missed. Sukey could handle filling their ale pots.

A couple of drovers were playing cribbage at one table. In another dark corner probity had returned; neither Dr. Prescott nor Maid Mulliken, nor the poor lonely scone were sitting there. The candle burned to nearly a nub and soon would leave the booth in even darker vacancy. Damn, not crowded enough, someone was bound to notice her absence.

Maybe send Sukey down the road.

One look at her Negro dispelled any notion of sending the poor girl. Too distraught. She was cleaning dishes and rinsing in a bucket, muttering, "Funeral, soldiers, soldiers, funeral…"

Nothing to do but wait. Mary began to help with the ale pots. "Early to bed tonight Sukey, tomorrow may come faster than we know."

The slave girl's eyes narrowed with dread. "And Funerals…"

Chapter Ten: Road to Folly Pond

Midnight Onwards
Hither and Yon Lexington & Environs
The Menotomy Road
The Bedford and Billerica Road

The horse was tired. Mr. Paul felt the animal beneath him trying hard, breath ragged.

At every farmyard or cottage, Good Rose's rasping breath and loud hoof-beats had fired the houselights, woken the neighbors, raised the dead. How many had man and beast roused this night? Ten doors? Twenty gates? Thirty barns? Mr. Paul lost count. But after the thud of horseshoes and the hiss of a whisper, the country was alive in every direction, a frantic circus of action in the horse's dust.

Aye, even after midnight – each dwelling summarily spurred to action, men and women were weighing arms and ammunition, filling powder horns, checking flintlock and folding bits of wadding.

All men kept a handful of prepared cartridges in the house, with pellets instead of ball – for the turkey or the fox – and one or two with ball for deer. But not enough for battle. Tight barrels or powder horns of gunpowder stayed dry, while paper cartridges in ammo pouches, vulnerable to the damp.

So, everyone set about preparing ball and cartridge, many hands making light work. But at this time of night, breathlessly fussing over paper, powder and thread – a rushed job was time consuming and worse – dangerous. No one in their right mind wants to work near open powder by the light of a hearth fire or a dozen candles. But you couldn't do it in the dark of a nighttime room.

Iron out the paper, cut lengths of thread. Fashion a cylinder.

Flatten one end, place the ball. Pour in three inches of powder. Fold the open end. Pack the cartridge, tie off the ball to secure it inside the cylinder. So, when you rammed the cartridge home, hopefully the paper wouldn't break.

Every little cartridge, a job of work.

Now do another and another as dawn steadily approached.

How many could frantic hands make? How fast? Enough to fill a cartridge pouch. Thirty? Forty? Like the old Proverb said about mending holes in rended garments, a stitch in time saved nine. Make your stitches early before the trouser holes spread so large you couldn't fix them.

Carpe Noctem. Seize the night.

The real trick was to avoid the suddenchance that Haste Makes Waste. Roll a paper cylinder, fold the end to seal one it, then make every twist and knot of the thread count. Worried every second a candle might fall over or paper catch. Somehow avoid blowing up the kitchen table in a fiery cloud of,

Egads and little fishes –

Kaboom!

Slow down. Hurry up. Slow down. This exhortation and admonition became the rule of the moment in every kitchen and parlor. Slow down. Hurry up. Slow down. As the candles burned and the night grew long.

Yet how could the good horse Rose know the rule of the moment in every house and kitchen? The gentle mare oblivious to any danger within a dwelling, the man half expecting to hear the whoosh and bang as he rode up the door or window along the way. But he too sensed the moment, riding both fast and slow. Hurry up. Slow down. The night seemed to lengthen with every league.

Inevitably the horse flagged as the road twisted and turned. Let good Rose rest a minute then, there'd be more riding soon. Lexington up ahead, Concord further on. No more spurs. His mount seemed to sigh in thanks and slowed to a walk. Better rest her before the final push.

Then all at once the trees and hedges parted. Low stone walls girded the Menotomy Road. The village Lexington sprang out of nowhere; at first a few cottages, then then proper houses. A stable. A store. Further in there'd be the Buckman Tavern off the Commons triangle, but he wouldn't push on that far. Not yet. Better check on the Parsonage.

Couldn't take the chance there'd be a squad of Lobsters camping out. Better to go around. Walk the horse quietly behind the Buckman dwelling, through the trees and back gardens. Might be too late already, but the sound of horse's hoof falls seemed so loud.

Back of the tavern a few small windows showed flickers of candlelight. And a few rough voices of ale sots thick with drink. The thrum of midnight voices. Some passionate, others almost frantic. The tavern full even now? So, word had already spread.

More low sounds came from the Commons. A random patrol?

No, not Redcoats, not in Lexington yet. Still, a low rumble of voices came from a dozen or so men milling about in the Commons. Some stretching out on the grass, others going back and forth into the tavern with tankards and leather bottles in their fists for post-midnight refreshment. So, news traveled fast. And for men prepared to wait out the night, even faster. The main body of the King's troops must be hours behind.

And these fellows camping out.

Waiting for a reckoning at dawn then.

Finally, the Parsonage appeared off to one side. A well-kept village house set back from the road overlooking a sturdy low wall. Like nearly every home in New England, the two-story parsonage was made of rocks and stones pulled from every field. Not an acre of ground in this hard land didn't have to be cleared of plow breakers. And so, walls, walls, walls for every homestead or plot. The house's curtains were drawn, but slivers of candlelight flickered from within.

Watchful.

Mr. Paul let his horse slow to a walk, hoofs scattering the white pebbles of the front yard. The man dismounted and the animal snorted with relief. The front door cracked an inch and a gruff voice sputtered, "Shhhhhh! No disturbance, no noise!"

One of Hancock's men – Sgt. Munroe – a pug-faced man wedged himself in the doorway, barring the way.

Mr. Paul snorted louder than the horse, "I'll give you noise! You'll have noise enough before long. The Regulars are on your doorstep!"

An upstairs window slammed open and Handsome John's strong voice plunged down, "Come in Revere, we're not afraid of you!"

The faces of Handsome John and Lawyer Adams appeared in different

Parsonage windows like twin full moons, one upstairs, one downstairs, their pale faces framed by curtains. The two rebel leaders looked down into the yard as if waiting for the two horsemen to do something, anything. Saddle up, ride off, or just walk away.

The bulldog sergeant Munroe harrumphed indulgently and let the rider over the threshold into the darkened house.

The long figure of Handsome John met him coming down the stairs. "Your commons is a campgrounds, Sir," Mr. Paul told him.

"Well, we're not going to tell our folk to go home. Are you?" This, from a short stubby man sitting quietly in front of the dead fireplace. A voice out of the shadows. A bit of balding head caught a sliver of light from the open door.

"Find your wig, Lawyer Adams, you shine like a moon. If the Lobsters take you, you'll need it for your first court appearance."

"I'll pack it for the crossing to London and the hangman. Let not my bald pate amaze you. Ride on, sir. Ride on."

Mr. Paul needed no more encouragement and made ready to leave without another word. But paused as yet a second rider, rode out of the gloom. Another messenger from Boston. The stern figure of Major Dawes leaned down from a tired horse; his face pockmarked with sweat. The Major rode the longer route – South down the causeway and Boston Neck – by land not sea.

The two riders paused for a moment in the yard. The extra few miles took a toll. A silent decision was made to wait for a spell. The minute man's horse was all done in, and Mr. Paul's good Rose could use a half hour off the saddle. With any luck this respite would let the horses refresh and gain a second wind.

The two messengers made no effort to go; instead they quietly sat on a wall. The horsemen weren't going anywhere while their mounts rested. Major Dawes pulled out a pipe and sucked on the dead stem, while the two animals nosed about looking for tufts of grass in the henpecked yard.

A servant quietly came from inside the Parsonage bearing tankards to the two men, ale, and water. And the two scouts drank deep of both, spilling some across their chins and onto the ground.

When a half hour passed, they tightened the girths on their horses again.

Slowly, the horsemen walked their mounts down the road leaving the midnight rumble of Buckman Tavern behind. They left the restless men on the commons to their night of watchfulness and the two Provincial headmen, Hancock and Adams in their parsonage to their own devices.

Clouds passed over the moon and dark engulfed the riders. Mounting their horses now, they urged their animals to a brisk trot, and from there into an uncertain future. The riders' unspoken thoughts – wondering the obvious – how many more of us? How many others might be riding out into the night to spread the word? Messengers, sentinels, scouts, anyone with two eyes and two legs? Doubtless the word would spread like the pox, except instead of sickening and killing people, the spreading alarums, would race into people's hearts and veins like a stiff drink. Bringing every woman and man jack out of their hidey holes.

And what of the King's men? Sturdy boots, tramping inland under relentless command. Dogged Lobsters under implacable orders of men both distant and close with no regard for consequences. Would they sense the seething throngs that surrounded them even as they marched from Boston?

Damned if either horse or rider knew. But two irreconcilable forces were gathering in the night, and like a pounding surf on a rocky shore, one would break upon the other and retreat back into the sea from which it came.

Perhaps no wiser for all that.

The pox-faced moon peeked down at them like an old crone hiding behind a fluttering Chinese fan. The Menotomy Road momentarily lit, a sullen slash between fields and copses, then vanished to black. Some ways behind, another set of hoofbeats faintly echoed out of the dark. A new man coming up, riding fast, the growing drumbeat of an approaching rider.

What to do? What to –

Take cover in a thicket?

Plunge ahead?

Let him come. A lone Lobster scout of no consequence. He could be defied or ignored. In twenty heartbeats, the rider came out of the dark and pulled abreast of the others. A wave of relief. Nothing to fear.

Only young Dr. Prescott.

To those overtaken in the dead of night, Major Dawes and Mr. Paul – young Dr. Prescott's cravat appeared hurriedly tied, and a smudge of … was that lip rouge? The rogue, playing in the heather when there was business to be done. The riders slowed to a walk.

The young Doctor seemed undone; his hat cocked sideways. Whether from riding hard or other exertions earlier in the night, hard to say. Amorous labors of an evening can take a toll on a young man. The lovers' stumbling tiptoe through field and hedgerow, from Hartwell Tavern to Miss Mulliken's house in Lexington earlier that evening gave moment to opportunity. The young lass and her swain clung to each other and paused once again to embrace, to paw and strain thigh to thigh. Then restrain once more.

Yet like all matters of the heart and other human parts –

Virtue is as virtue does.

Lydia and Prescott forsook the open ground for the unoccupied Mulliken house – empty for the moment, quitting the damp night grass for an hour alone on a settee in the parlor. A plain, Quaker kind of loveseat, with hard bottom cushion and not much backing. Forcing lover's exertions awkwardly undone, hand, hook and buttons. Moments of protest, them mewing consent. But once undone, not as easily returned to presentable appearance.

"You look like a man interrupted, Doctor," growled Major Dawes.

"Not so much interrupted as spent, Sir. I heard you passing as I was taking my leave of – "

"Say no more," the Major raised an open hand. "A gentleman never tells." All agreed, silently nodding in assent. As far as men of honor were concerned, lovers' tales were best ignored.

"You've heard the news?"

"No, but you seem like men roused and without a spare minute between you. I can guess the news. General Gage marching his Regulars deep into the country by silent drum."

The horses nodded their heads as if in agreement.

The riders dug their spurs and quickened the pace. The houses came and went, front yards, back yards, doors knocked, windows opened and hurriedly shut, hurriedly lit candles as hurriedly blown out, many heads in nightcaps and rumpled night gowns, there were men they caught snoring and women they caught on the loo, many more half-dressed, chuckling in stitches as they buttoned their britches – a church bell here, a raised voice there – even another lovers' interruption. This time a certain Mister Baker and a certain Miss Taylor.

Dr. Prescott himself thundered up to one household door, "Come along, Mr. Baker. Your duty to Miss Taylor is done for the night!" The arduous Mr. Baker, a fellow of fair appearance, tumbled out the door as another virtuous daughter of liberty handed him a brace of pistols, belt, sash and saber. The unflappable Miss Taylor helping him to the stable as he dropped one thing after another, her picking it up and strapping it about him as they made their way on.

The man's horse waiting patiently under a lean-to looked skeptically at the approaching fussy clucks. As if to say, humans.

While the hurried Mr. Baker merely called over his shoulder, "I kept her bridled and saddled!"

"Very prudent," Dr. Prescott muttered. Then louder, "We're on to Folly Pond, to Concord. And you?"

"Hither and yon, in and out," the bumbling Baker replied. "Everywhere and anywhere. Should we part, know me when you see me."

Chapter Eleven: Midnight Ride

April 19th, 2:00 AM
Menotomy Road
Folly Pond

The love-muddled Mr. Baker – no longer a Colonial Casanova – had shed the guise of Romeo and was now clear of purpose. The young minute man hurtled off on horseback to warn family and friends, and every Lincoln-County-Son either side of Menotomy Road. By crossing back and forth over the thoroughfare, in a ragged zig zag he covered more than a night's work across town and county.

The original horsemen – Major Dawes, young Doctor Prescott and Mr. Paul – kept to their original course, pressing on to Concord. Whether under moonlight or dark clouds, the wind and sky overhead ignored them, sometimes shining light, other times cloaking them against all eyes. A ribbon of silver when the moon shone down, then ribbon of black as the moon hid her face. The three riders devoured the ground as they rode the pike. First, through Lincoln County, then cantering on towards the little body of water called Folly Pond – but still far from Concord.

At first all went well. The dwellings on either side of the road roused and ready, lights burning in the windows. The riders passed them by with a shout and a wave. But then came a dark stretch between homesteads. A gentle curve in the road that blocked sight of the way ahead. Mr. Paul urged his horse forward, gaining ground, a hundred yards, two hundred. The others spurred their mounts to catch him. But all were riding blind.

As Mr. Paul reached a bend in the road, he spied the flat black water of Folly Pond like a pool of oil on the ground. Close by, a lone tree grew by the path. The overhanging tree branches threw midnight shade about the road. A low field wall and a split-rail gate rose up out of nowhere to hem them in. Two of the three gate rails lay on the ground, easy to jump, no barrier between field or road.

But under those dark branches of the tree stood the motionless figures of two more horsemen. Soldier sentinels. Scouts marched out from Charlestown.

King's men.

Mr. Paul's mount, good Rose, came scattering to a halt with scraping hooves and a wet snort. Seeing the lurkers Mr. Paul shouted over his shoulder, "Here are two of them!" With his companions riding hard behind, now it was three rebels against two royal scouts. Three against two. Good odds.

King's men were prize captures. Unhorse them, bind their hands, blindfold them with neckerchiefs – then spin them round like blind man's bluff. Once thoroughly disoriented, you'd mount them again and lead them around all night by their horses' halters, through bog, and fen and tangle. An hour, two hours, all night long. Then unhorse the redcoats once more and whip the beasts down the road bareback. By dawn the King's men would be so lost it would take them half the morning just to find their bearings. While the horses wandered back to their stable, without a whinny of compliance at the night's frolics.

The rebels liked to call this turnaround game, "Hold for Questioning." Though no one ever got questioned; they played it just to keep the King's men dizzy and confused. And they'd always let the Lobsters go, back to barracks or Boston command to report the shame of being captured.

"We'll hold them for questioning," Mr. Paul hollered, "till the troubles pass – fair or foul!" A few scouts missing from the General's main body of soldiery could only make things more difficult for the redcoats. And so, it might have gone if not for chance and fickle fate – the King's men were reinforced.

The fantasized prize of captured horsed scouts vanished in a twinkling.

Even as Mr. Paul scuffled to seize a King's man – more Lobsters approached from the pasture, beyond the gate. Their mounts hopped the dropped bar and now four horsemen encircled the one left in the middle of the road. Both Mr. Paul and young Doctor Prescott caught unawares, abroad at night, bang to rights. Abroad at night. For what nefarious purpose?

Sneaky thieves clearly up to their eyes in rebellion.

Both rebel and redcoats knew what they were about.

Nothing good.

To alarm every man jack in Massachusetts the King's troops were on the march. To stir up the populace into frothing rage –

A saber loosed from scabbard with a bold swoosh. Pistols drawn, then cocked. That hammer clank, a dangerous sound.

"Damn you, stop!" one of the Crown's men shouted. "Go an inch further, you're a dead man!"

Major Dawes – furthest behind – reined his horse around made off at a high gallop. Yet another Boston rebel worth pursuing. Two of the King's men went after him.

Now it was just two against two once more. Young Prescott came to Mr. Paul's aid, flailing the butt of his whip at their captors. But no good – riders against riders – the King's men forced the young Doctor and Mr. Paul over the dropped rails and into the pasture.

Nothing for it but cut and run.

Young Prescott dashed off towards the edge of the field and yet over another stone wall. His horse leapt the barrier, and the two Lobsters followed close behind.

Suddenly alone, Mr. Paul dashed away in the opposite direction towards the safety of some woods. But no sooner had he reached the trees, six more Lobsters appeared out of the dark. Hands grabbed his bridle, and more than one pistol touched his chest.

One officer came from behind, rode close and bid the others put away their firearms. Prim, shaven and direct, his buttons gleamed like silver in the moonlight. He seemed a courteous man, and inquired politely, "Travel far? Where did you come from?"

"Boston," the reply.

"Sir, may I crave your name?

"My name is Revere."

Taken aback the prim and proper officer couldn't help but shake the reins, "What!" startling his horse.

The horse settled and the King's officer spoke slowly. "Paul Revere." And savored the words in his mouth as a revelation.

"Yes."

At once the other five Lobsters jostled in close, angry, threatening. One ugly face after another thrust forward or lips curled back in promised vengeance.

"Ship him to England!"

"Passage the hold."

"Gibb'um the fokhsul!"

And with each shout Mr. Paul's poor horse whipped her head this way and that but couldn't get from the hands at her bridle. Then began to buck and whinny.

But the prim and proper officer would have none of this. With a stern look at his rough men, they quieted down. Then to Mr. Paul, "Fear not. No one shall hurt you."

The rebel was the prize, and he knew it.

The officer's rough soldiers reluctantly stood down, still muttering. But fell silent in dismay when they saw their comrades returning from across the pasture. Alone.

The King's men failed to capture the one who fled. No young Doctor Prescott.

The soldiers' horses were covered in mud. Chasing the young man along the edge of a muck pool then into thickets – between mud and gorse bushes – somehow, they'd lost their quarry. The soldiers returned empty-handed, with that long look of defeat that starts in a man's shoulders and bends his spine. Knowing full well the young Doctor was still free as a bird to sound alarums. Crestfallen, they returned to their station by the fallen gate under the shadows of the tree.

Mr. Paul tried not to seem too pleased.

"Ah well, Gentleman – you've missed your aim." The warning bells and morning drums would not be silenced round the countryside.

The prim and proper officer looked long and deeply down a long thin nose. Unruffled by the prospect of loose men warning Concord, he coolly lied about his purpose with a gentle voice.

"Not at all, Sir. No, we shall not."

He looked in the direction of Boston, explaining drolly, "We are only waiting for some deserters we expect along the road. They'll be for the forecastle if Gage doesn't hang them in Boston Commons."

But Mr. Paul could not contain a chuckle.

"Sir, I know better." He waved an arm across the sky, the road, the fields. "We know what you are after, guns and patriots. But be warned. I've raised the alarm. The countryside knows of you in every direction. I saw your men run aground in Charlestown's muddy banks."

Mr. Paul glanced at his seized pistol in the other's hand. "If our people weren't already up, I'd have risked a shot at you just to warn them. There'll be five hundred Americans here."

The officer looked disdainfully at the empty fields, the scudding moon and all the quiet of a country night, only the peepers in the fields singing for each other.

"Sir, mud or no mud, we will have fifteen hundred regulars along shortly."

And with that, he signaled more men in the black shadow of a copse, four horsemen with three others, each afoot, hands tied and tethered to a King's horse.

Three more Provincials captured that night. They looked extremely ill-used. Cocked hats, beaten and askew, black lumps about their faces where they'd been questioned harshly.

The King's officer turned horse around, leaving Mr. Paul to his ruffians. Then galloped to the road to bring those standing under the tree for extra guard. Returning in force the King's men were none too happy. Another officer, a Major, still wet from clapping about the muck and mire, and losing young Dr. Prescott was in no mood for games. A cold and angry man, the Major put his pistol to Mr. Paul's head and demanded in all certainty of outcome, "You'll answer us now. And if you do not tell the truth, you'll be looking for your head."

There's a moment of calm when a man knows he may be for it. Mr. Paul looked down at his hands for the tell-tale trembles. Nothing. Only thing to do was breathe.

"I esteem myself a man of truth, Sir."

"Esteem what you like," the officer growled.

"You've jacked me on the highway by force of arms, by might not right. Yet I will tell the truth."

And again, the officer battered him with questions, about supplies, the magazine at Concord, Rebel guards, bridges cleared or blocked – getting no further than before. Mr. Paul was under no obligation to tell them of Handsome Hancock and Mr. Adams, back in Lexington. For all he knew, those two had moved on into the hinterlands far from Royal prerogative.

Disgusted and resigned, both officers and King's Lobsters, bade their prisoner's horses brought out and all mounted. When Mr. Paul touched his reins, the cold Major took them from his hands and gave them to the kindly officer to lead them. "By God, sir we'll not have you ride with reins, of that you can be sure."

Mr. Paul's horse tethered to another's pommel left no room for flight. Then all the soldiers formed a rough circle of their prisoners, pushing Mr. Paul to the front. They clopped back towards Lexington with the final warning –

"At the first attempt to run, at the first insult, the hammer falls. We'll splatter your brains over your horse's neck."

They had their opportunity soon enough. But not with Mr. Paul. With another. Passing a house on the road, a fellow burst out the front door.

The excited fellow shouting, "What news? What news?"

While his wife, wiser than him by leagues called, "Josiah come back inside! Come back!"

Rushing toward the line of horses, not realizing his mistake, Josiah presented himself for reprimand. Indeed, even before noticing the redcoats under their blue cloaks. And realizing his error, too late, too late. No, the British weren't going tell him anything about their movements.

The bumptious fool a worthy target, a redcoat saber flashed out of its scabbard and banged him with the ricasso edge of the blade. Not enough to cleave the man's skull but enough to knock him down, break the skin and make him bleed.

Thence staggering back into the clucking arms of a wiser wife, while the echo of church bells rang into the night.

Chapter Twelve: Buttered Rum

Mary Hartwell
Captain Smith's Farmhouse
What Young Brown Saw

Captain Smith's farmhouse wasn't half a mile away. Best start there. Mary Hartwell's sturdy footfalls on the road were swallowed up into the sky. The night air a tonic after the smoky tavern. Though Mary couldn't see the pink and white blossoms in the dark, their clean scent filled her head. The breeze picked up and she heard the flutter of leaves and the gentle kiss of flying blossoms across her cheek.

The Captain's house loomed out of the dark. Door open, lantern windows lit. She saw his round figure in the doorway, candle in hand.

"Come in out of the dark and we'll settle up." The Captain moved aside to let Mary through into the kitchen. "I've had news all night!"

A round, short man, all waistcoat, breeches and boots – he seemed to fill the entranceway, then the low kitchen. A low fire burned in the stone hearth; the scent of cinnamon and clove and butter wafted under her nose. Mary saw a copper pitcher by the fire, with a trace of steam rising from it.

Buttered rum.

The Captain's breath thick with it. Where in heaven's name had the old badger gotten Rum? And Sugar? There'd been none since forever. The smell of buttered rum got stronger as he spoke.

"Take a draught, Mary. I've been saving a five-gallon cask for months.

Came down from Rhode Island, a smuggler's wreck. Liberated a dozen barrels off a King's man merchant from Medford. Sold the other eleven casks back to the Loyalists in Boston. Serve them right."

For a moment, Mary wondered if the would-be smuggler sold his swag to the sad and handsome Lieutenant; then realizing immediately, that stern British officer would not be trifled. He'd arrest the mercenary Captain as soon as look at him. And she felt a touch of admiration. The unyielding rule and unbending will of a man clothed in a red coat.

"Yes, Captain," the sarcasm rose like bile. "You made quite a killing, selling them back to Loyals. Who sell it for even more to the Lobsters in Red. While my tavern sells homemade swill. Thank you kindly."

Captain Smith took a deep, buttered breath, his cheeks merry as Father Christmas. "But you're an honest tavern, Mary. And you be selling rum you'd have Redcoats camping in your parlor."

Mary shrugged, "They camp there anyway. A squad of Lobsters passed by my place, not half an hour ago, heading back to town."

The Captain nodded sagely, took a big swig of his tankard. Then a blast of buttered rum as he spoke.

"Saw 'em. Trying to be sly and slip past. But I saw 'em!"

Mary didn't think the soldiers had been particularly sly or shy – just slow riders. Executing a strange, dubious tactic patrolling the backcountry. To be seen and not be seen. That was the object. To be seen so as to intimidate, but not be seen, so as to come upon plotters, smugglers, and the Minutemen unawares.

Another blast of buttered rum. "Busy night. Gonna get busier still!" The captain took the warm copper from the hearth and ladled Mary a dollop in a small clay pot. While the night's doings poured out of him in after each swallow and Mary listened trying to make sense of it all –

There'd been comings and goings since early afternoon. A young man by the name of Brown had come up from Boston market, walking the ten miles in broad daylight under the cover of absolutely nothing. Footloose and carefree, young Brown made a spectacle of himself, tipping his hat to every rider, strider and milking cow chewing her cud along the road. As he strode along, the fellow went out of his way to knock winter's dried thistle heads off stalks. The dried stalks made a nice clean clacking sound with each strike of Young Brown's walking stick. The noise getting the attention of anyone tending a yard, tilling a field or behind an open kitchen window, eager to hear the news.

Foolish or clever? A little of both.

Young Brown's sharp eye had seen the Redcoat patrols ride out, saw the King's men go round and round. He'd seen the brass and silver butt-plates of their pistol hafts and the shiny metal of their saber guards. Telling anyone who would listen just that – and many did – including the rum-buttered Captain Smith.

Yes, the regulars were coming. On their way.

There were others watching too and sending messages of their own.

Every milkmaid, every farmer driving a plow, every peddler, every servant feeding hens by the barn – anyone with two eyes or an eyepatch.

Even the Committee for Safety back in Boston, at the Black Horse Tavern had dispatched a rider. A rider from that nest of rebels bending elbows, Handsome John Hancock and all his worthies holding forth under wafting tavern smoke, tankard and clay pipe.

Where yet another committee, the committee of supplies, under the horrid name, Secret Committee of Congress – busily decided where to keep their stock and stores, their material, where to hide their cannon, shot and powder. Prattling on about their own salaries – how much to pay each other – whether by rank or by exalted social position or local militia. Arguing over any and every other particular.

Did these talkative men even take a vote on sending riders out to Lexington? Or just call, "Ride out, Sir. Ride out!"

Neither Captain Smith nor innkeeper Mary knew. And neither cared. Yet this same Committee's rider saw eight or nine Lobsters in a patrol heading inland, west. But if these were the very redcoats that Captain Smith, Brown and Mary Hartwell saw going back the other way – none could say.

Confusion ruled the night and day.

Chapter Thirteen: Dark March Dark Thoughts

Menotomy Road Inland
Searching nighttime barns and farms
To No Avail

The night wore on, booted feet tramping through the dark. The good and patient Belle followed Lieutenant Moreau without complaint; the officer had dismounted hours ago and led Belle with barely a tug. Always up for a rainy-day ride or a walk on a fine night, the good Belle followed her reins draped over her master's shoulder.

The peaceful horse followed her master, content to walk through the night as the clock marched toward dawn. Lieutenant Moreau's troop had pitchforked more hayricks, banged on more doors, scandalized more farmers' wives in their nightgowns than any could remember. Farmhouse, barn, henhouse, pig-pen, farmhouse, barn again, from one domicile to another looking for stores and stolen swag. But the Provincials had done their work too well. Two days earlier at least. Every flat pallet, every shack with a roof picked clean, their precious goods moved to safety.

It didn't take Lieutenant Moreau's experienced eye to see some cavernous, empty barn packed to the rafters not 36 hours earlier. An overloaded store-room – casks marked RUM against one wall. Kegs of gunpowder, marked with skull and crossbones, some painted red, oak and reinforced, stacked against every wall. A horse stall packed tight with muskets, another with a hundred powder horns hanging by their straps, and shelves of premade boxes of paper cartridges. A full storeroom of food, arms and supplies.

Yet no homestead, shed or barn showed anything but cornhusks, strewn straw, flattened pinecones and the fallen leaves of winter.

No molasses, no gunpowder, no stocks of muskets or loaves of sugar.

Yet the barn floor still told a different story. Wagon wheel tracks heading out, deep grooves – cannon or gun carriage ruts? Even a blind man could see it.

When Moreau stood on the empty floorboards or dirt floor, he could imagine Revere the Silversmith standing there. In the dark as now, as the long shadows consumed every wall and window, the Silversmith standing there like a wooden Indian patiently watching. While that hussy from the tavern, Mary something, quietly gave orders. Mary Hart-something, Hartwell, yes, he'd already marked her in his book … the day he helped her with the hand-cart. Using the good Belle to useful effect, lightening the woman's burdens, and hopefully showing some kindness to the rising storm of anger. Pouring oil on the waters. For all the good it did. From that moment forward, Moreau couldn't manage to forget her. A sturdy and handsome woman, the bold and competent face of the New World. And then he immediately regretted the thought.

Meg, Mayfair. Something better in London.

Yet the image of the self-sufficient Yankee lady persisted in his mind. Her bodice, half-laced, a sheen of sweat between her breasts. The capable, determined face ordering men about. How unlike the pale and frail Meg. The bold Yankee woman persisting on and on – on placement, on disbursement, on the evacuation of goods to places known and unknown:

"Corn sacks to Broker's farm.

"We're going to need another wagon for the powder. Check Clintwell's yard.

"Hitch the Tavern's horses for the gun carriage.

"Try Fernman's farm, eight miles northwest – and not his main barn, the shed in the woods by the thickets near the swamp. The one no one knows is there.

Many hands made light work. More men than women? Or more women than men? Even in his imagination, Lieutenant Moreau could not really tell.

That popinjay Hancock had sent a few of his pirates too. Grizzled sailors three days away from their last shave and threadbare in their appearance. Still, the ruffians helped with the steady, methodical emptying of every nook and cranny, sacks of wheat and flour, helpful bodies coming and going, tread and footprints by scores of boots and hooves – stooping for smaller loaves of precious sugar, cradled in comforting arms like little babies -- used as much for barter as for coffee and cake, better than coin and better than currency.

And there in the middle of the floor, the prize of prizes – the brass field piece, 3-pound galloper and five brass monkeys each filled with a four-by-four pyramid of cannon balls. Thirty balls per brass monkey, one hundred fifty cannonballs all told. Enough powder and shot for a three-hour bombardment. This gun, one of four stolen guns. Stolen right out from under their noses, and under guard.

Had the redcoat sentries been bribed? Drunk on duty?

Moreau never found out. A few soldiers had been brought before a Courts Martial. But the outcome was unknown. Deserters? The officer in charge of total dereliction of duty – hailed from highborn connections so there were no consequences for him.

Whose bastard highborn scion, Moreau did not know. Only that the guns were spirited away – "gallopers" they were called as a mule or a nag or a couple of healthy mares could pull them hither and yon with the barest effort.

Standing in the empty barn of his mind, Moreau heard the faint echo of wagon wheels and gun carriages, that tell-tale rattle of wheeled bronze, brass and iron retreating into the dark. A staccato cadence of highway robbery, rattling off into the distance. Each thump and clatter, the echo of battle, distant thunder, a promise for later –

A reckoning.

Somewhere out in the future, but coming, coming soon.

But it wasn't just that trollop – Inn-Keep Tavern Mary – who took a hand in this highway robbery of artillery – no … long before the forced march, the swim in the Charles, the lugging of the boats, the wet on the bank, before all that there'd been a whisper, a little tale told, another woman weighing her clout against the Crown.

Another woman, half American half Brit, more influential than a tavern keeper's hussy – General Gage's own bedmate.

The great man's spouse, woman, wife – there'd been rumors and bad talk among the ranks in the barracks for months. Born in New Brunswick, could the high-born courtesan really be trusted? Doubts chalked up as graffiti in alleyways and on outhouse walls, a sordid tale – the infamous jade Mrs. Margaret

Kemple – a crude rendering of dress, bodice and grotesque face, with a stick figure forcing his male member in her mouth, the caption, "She swallowed the full Hancock, General Gage."

Awful cartoons, graffiti, and illiterate scrawls scribbled on every surface that could take chalk. The "Hancock" member had made the rounds from pillar to post. And General Gage could only bring water and brush to bear. American born and yet she married – of course Moreau had heard the rumors. Army Rumors – of the woman's cunny liberality.

Margaret Kemple's favorites or "lovers" – the rumored ardent swains – gallant officers who by social position courted her as drones to a queen bee. Some officers too handsome for their own good, others clearly ugly ducklings in hopes that her merest attention might turn them into a favored swan.

Lieutenant Moreau knew two of those officers well enough to nickname them.

There was Major Toad, a pox-faced simpering, obsequious fellow in his late 40s. His commission bought and paid for, but without any real chance of advancement, for he had little originality and less verve. Moreau had never seen him under fire, as the Major preferred instead to remain on the command line or command tent whenever the business of soldiering became serious.

Long abandoned on the road to promotion, the pock-faced officer now bowed and scraped wherever required. His uniforms, however, were stunningly crafted by the best tailors in London. Now, in the colonies when a tear or open seam threatened his appearance, Major Toad went into a fit of panic searching for a seamstress. The man was easily recognizable with a scrap of cockade in his tri-corner hat, bright yellow, of no other significance that he could be picked out in a throng through the spyglass, if ever he unluckily found himself in the heat of battle, or in the horse-charged, unbreathable, sulfurous fog of war.

Captain Fink on the other hand fancied himself the Prussian soldier in every regard. Handsome as a sharpened knife. Younger than Lieutenant Moreau his exalted family connections guaranteed a spot on the general's staff, but he preferred front line duty. Ordinarily Moreau would have admired this – but the necessary skill of making command decisions rendered the poor young officer invertebrate.

Like many a bold ambitious fellow his courage ran supple. More afraid of making a mistake Captain Fink often waffled. Easy enough for Lieutenant Moreau to simply stand by and obey foolish, contradictory orders. What was harder to stomach were no orders at all. The clock became your enemy, while a real opponent lurked or maneuvered close at hand. It was Moreau's bad luck to be under Fink's command on a training march to scout the nearby villages and hamlets some months earlier.

General Gage had issued orders, *"If any Officers of the different Regiments are capable of taking sketches of a Country, they will send their names to the Deputy Adjutant General*." At the time it struck Moreau a peculiar way of wording the order, as if Gage had little or no faith there was even one officer under his command capable of walking out into the adjacent fields, copses, roads or hamlets and making a damn map. Sail a thousand miles and not one mapmaker in their ranks? Apparently, they had left the screever on the docks at Portsmouth.

Captain Fink, however, had studied some art in London at a salon and fancied he knew his way around a map-case and rolled paper. Volunteering for "sketching" duty in early January, he marched a troop out into the countryside. It had snowed for three days and everywhere they turned a frozen mess presented itself, before sleighs could tamp down the roads. Occasionally, they had to ford a stony bit of creek or circumvent a swamp clogged with frozen leaves.

Slippery, cold, Captain Fink split up the men under his command. Moreau commanded an ensign with the Frenchified name of De Bernière, a bright young fellow with a good hand on parchment. While Captain Fink went off with Sergeant Muggs, a stout, honest fellow, but with a thick scruff of 2-day old beard on his cheeks that made one immediately think of a Barbary ape.

The detail went out the Menotomy Road, dressed in brown clothes, indistinguishable from any countryman or peddler. Except that each man was issued a red kerchief. Why? Moreau had no idea, so they might recognize each other in a crowd. There would be few crowds on the country roads and in the hamlets. But a man, however sensibly disguised with folder and sketch book would be as easily noticed as a hairy wen on a noble nose.

Indeed, how to make sketches presented its own problems. From areas of concealment, naturally. For who wanted to attract attention by standing in the middle of a thoroughfare drawing maps with pencil or charcoal? It wasn't as though this were French Provence where people stood in fields of lavender to paint the scenery.

This was grim New England in Winter. Cold, bitter, suspicious, and hard underfoot as any January in Hell.

Lieutenant Moreau recalled how Captain Fink's detail split up before Concord, pledging on the return to meet again at the Charleston docks for a row across the Charles back to Boston.

Lieutenant Moreau and Ensign De Bernière for their part made maps as they could, hiding in bushes, where the bare thickets were thickest, behind wagons frozen in the mud and ditches where they couldn't be spotted. Avoiding the warmth of taverns and houses and the like, finding the occasional abandoned barn awaiting springtime and kinder climes. Over the course of a day the brown clad soldiers filled a map-case with a rolled wad of sketches.

At the Charleston docks some hours later, Lieutenant Moreau and De Bernière waited. Waited and waited long into a bitter January night. Until halfway through the clock, Captain Fink appeared alone.

Explaining dismally, "I've lost Muggs. The Sergeant took it on himself to do a go-round a swamp, I didn't order it. And slipped and fell and twisted an ankle and now he's sitting on the side of the road five miles up. I think we need a cart."

Lieutenant Moreau and Ensign De Bernière looked aimlessly about; no carts in sight. The nearest homestead might have a cart they could borrow.

"We'll find one, sir."

And so, they rented the horse cart from a sleepy local. Promising to return it afterwards, but instead forgetting entirely, and abandoning the cart by the dock as the three men leveraged Sgt. Muggs into a rowboat. Finally, returning Sgt. Muggs to the barracks where he belonged, well after dawn.

What did all this prove?

Only that the handsome, vacillating, well-connected, highborn Captain Fink misplaced the men under his command, couldn't make maps to save his life – and to Lieutenant Moreau's eternal contempt – still escaped reprimand and punishment from Regimental command. Life wasn't fair. And the military even less so.

This incident stuck in Lieutenant Moreau's craw – recalling it from January onward souring him. The knife of cynicism unsheathed once, was never to be returned to the scabbard. If he'd fully grasped it at the time, he would have thought to himself, "This is how deserters are created."

But thinking of deserting was a far cry from vacating the barracks with his trunk, sword, pistol, and haversack, with the good Belle in tow. And so, Lieutenant Moreau soldiered on as was his duty.

Foursquare on Mrs. Gage's side in all matters, even under persistent rumors of infidelity. Yes, he'd seen the great Lady for himself and knew the difference between sluts and nonsense. Mrs. Gage was elegant and modest and if she did divulge the whereabouts of the stolen cannon she did so out of the deepest conflict, not some lover's rutting. He had been privileged to help her once, by holding open a heavy door and escorting her into the light and gaiety of a party – and yet still misunderstandings came with every turn of the frock.

A Winter Ball – same early January as the incident with Captain Fink and his misplaced men.

But on the night of Mrs. Gage's party it was Major Toad's star turn on the stage of essential rear echelon operations. Captain Fink, Major Toad, Sergeant Muggs and Ensign De Bernière all found themselves that glittering night on parade, the welcoming squad at the entrance to Province House. And as all the worthies arrived by carriage, they brought up the rear like dutiful husbands, helping highborn women in wide gowns navigate the tricky icy steps. While Moreau found himself in charge of the door.

And it was under these particular circumstances that Lieutenant Moreau came to understand the importance of ladies' fashions and their role in history. General Gage, not to be outdone by royal visits, assigned his subalterns to helping each woman out of their conveyance. Carriage after carriage rolled down Marlborough Street, clattered to a halt before the long entrance stones to Province House. A double line of junior officers, Moreau among them, stood at parade on either side, as Mrs. G's guests walked the treacherous flagstones from cobblestoned street to grand entranceway stair. While above, the Indian Archer Weathervane atop the house turret swung haphazardly over the partygoers below, flittering in a bay breeze as if uncertain which way the winter weather might break.

Tonight, the air was cold and clear, with a gust of wind that tugged the coats and women hurried to the warmth and light of the house.

And here Moreau spied the most curious thing, Mrs. G's closest friend, Agnes Postrel – her coat tugged open by the wind as she hurried clutched it together, but not before Moreau saw the fabric of her gown. Blue satin and pale-yellow velvet in V-shaped stripes. It caught the light from the windows, and he remarked not only on how beautiful the colonial woman's Lady Virginia gown was, but something else entirely. Almost a twin to the gown Mrs. G wore for the ball. Yes, the stripes may have been a little wider, the velvet a little paler, yes one or the other of the women's petticoat a little bluer, but strikingly similar.

And Moreau knew without having to be told, this was no accident. Women never wore the same thing, and if such unlikely accident occurred it meant something. The candlelit ballroom glittered back at him. Not regal but more than pleasing to the eye, the very best of colonial gaiety –

The string Sextet was playing something, perhaps the Mozart waltz in F major, but at a faster pace. Both women – Lady Margaret Gage and her best friend Agnes Postrel were dancing and by trick of the eye, Moreau couldn't tell which was which, two women of similar dress, intermixed on the ballroom floor – confusing to the eyes, one dress for the other, one woman for the other.

But Moreau finally got a bead on one woman and caught the critical difference in their dance cards – the handsome Captain Fink danced with Lady Gage's best friend Postrel instead of Lady Gage herself. Yes, Lady Gage's favorite suitor, the handsome Captain Fink turning his attentions to a female rival. Trading one Lady Virginia gown for another, one dress for another.

Then gracefully twirling off the ballroom floor to a dark alcove. The Lieutenant stayed a safe distance away, as Postrel's flowing dress and the Captain's red coat briefly brushed up against each other. And he saw where soldier and twin sister touched hands, faces coming together. Postrel's face close to Captain Fink's – more than enough to birth rumors of infidelity in eyes hungry for scandal, and a few ugly strokes of graffiti in well-trod alleys. A distraction, a diversion from the real illicit tryst that night.

Lieutenant Moreau looked down from another dark alcove with a long-curtained window. In the even darker street in the walled garden behind the house, he saw what no one was supposed to see. The real business of Margaret Gage.

The General's wife, the genuine Margaret Gage in a similar gown and with yet another red coat.

Major Toad.

The two conspirators came together for a moment, not romantically, not intimately – but sober and business-like. A couple of words and a mutual nod of the head.

Yet for what? It could have been as innocent as asking to take a letter back home to England. Major Toad did not even take her hand to kiss it in obsequiousness, a cold formality stood between the two as they conducted their business. But as to the particulars, nothing could be known.

No, Major Toad was not groveling before the goddess Gage. But treating her as equal. A simple message from her husband General via the go-between Major? Some qualified treason? And no, this couldn't be about cannon.

A month earlier at Twelfth Night's end, those critical field pieces had already been stolen from the Castle of William and Mary – perhaps this secret rendezvous was about general supplies, or the desire for the whereabouts of high rebel leaders. Moreau could not say.

If Margaret Gage were indeed the one who let the whereabouts of the cannon slip out –

And thereby spirited away –

Or let her husband's plans be known, knowing his orders –

Whether glimpsed on his paper-strewn desk or whispered to her by some young admirer or even Major Toad –

She was not alone.

No, the leaks of information from British Regiment HQ dripped from Boston like water through a strainer. Trickles whispered from mouth to ear to mouth, sprayed by a messenger, rushing like a rider on a cart, from homestead, to tavern to Hancock and beyond. Information seemed to come from everywhere and nowhere like the biblical flood. Rumors existed on their own and were never to be resolved to anyone's satisfaction. Only teaching him once and for all to pay closer attention to the bows and bangles of a lady's dress.

Moreau understood only this:

The upper class was nothing if not upper in every way. Members of the fairer sex and the same strata did not bed stableboys, despite what the novelists would have you believe. But clearly, her American blood could not be married off…

This curious reality kept Lieutenant Moreau straddling the fence of indecision; was the General's Wife with them or against them? And her chaste tryst with Major Toad brought Moreau no closer to understanding.

Chapter Fourteen: Skirmish

Lexington Green

The eleven-mile march by Lieutenant Moreau's men settled in their soldiers' legs. A kind of slouch starting at the shoulders, clamping in around the thighs and ankles, making every man jack of them look a staggering ape.

A rest was ordered by command near a low stone wall along the road. This moment of respite might well have been the same field, the Lieutenant surveyed on that winter's day mapping with Ens. De Bernière. The Lieutenant's forethought in Boston getting his men to remove their socks before disembarkation had paid off well. The little difference of going barefoot off their boats to climb a mud bank of the Charles, putting on dry socks after drying their feet – more than worth the effort. During the interval Lieutenant Moreau heard no grumbles or complaints, just the sigh of taking a load off. Dry feet make for happier men. Less slog, more haste.

During this pause, a colonial rider, a rebel on a horse trotted near, then quickly turned his horse's nose, abruptly taking another route. Swinging his mount about, the rebel clattered off west. No one in Moreau's troop rose to chase the rider.

Why would they?

Militia and provincials were everywhere, and the King's men had lost the advantage of surprise long before they left Boston harbor. Yet another Rebel Monkey on horseback scampering off to tell his fellow monkeys in Lexington & Concord the devils were coming. Lieutenant Moreau sighed and motioned for his men to rise. In the dead hour before dawn Lexington was still nearly a mile away.

Another trudge.

Lieutenant Moreau's footsore marines emerged on the Lexington commons in good order. The rising sun at their backs threw long shadows at the soldiers' feet making phantom giants of mortal men. Rosy-fingered dawn had come like Homer, not by little caresses, but drawing open like the curtains in a theater. A blue veil in the East, gently raised. The clanging church bells that had followed them every mile of their march suddenly ceased. Leaving in their place an empty hollow silence, punctuated only by the shuffle of boots, the clank of arms and the grunts of men.

One minute dark, the next, sun lancing their backs in long beams of light, throwing daunting shadows at their feet. Other troops had already gathered on the commons, in more or less good order.

To say no one wanted battle was not strictly true. To say that no one wished to stay at home behind closed doors, not strictly true either. To say that all men in the field desired a bloody dawn not true at all. This was turf war. A standoff, a show of force. A skirmish to determine fleeting supremacy. If it had been located in the fair Carib, or the Gold Coast they might have called it a Bush War.

Major Pitcairn commanded the commons. Moreau got the distinct impression the Major recognized the faces of various Provincial rustics. Pointing with saber and calling out to his subalterns, "there's one to arrest, there's 'nother." And there seemed no lack of rebels in the morning light.

A cluster of men had gathered in front of the local saloon, the Buckman Tavern. Several score, first a dozen, then two dozen, then three dozen all coming out the low door of the alehouse, clutching pistol, musket and cutlass. How so many could emerge from the cramped saltbox on the green, Moreau couldn't say.

He'd been in the taproom once, a low-ceilinged, cramped dungeon, a fireplace and a kitchen. Before long, four score rebels stood before the clapboard tavern, some extra bodies coming from behind. Behold the local militia, Lexington's training band – a bumbling spawn of men and boys, all related to Captain Parker.

Inbreds.

But a mass of men nonetheless, daunting in their numbers. Eighty men standing together always looked impressive. At least for the first few minutes of martial display. Until the King's regulars arrived at ten times their number.

800 or so coming up the road and out of the woods on every side. Flanking troops converging on the same spot, the Lexington green. Now dwarfing the gaggle of men before Buckman Tavern.

When Pitcairn spotted Moreau's men coming out into the sunlight, he brightened considerably, waved a greeting to Moreau, and in salutation the Captain's voice rang across the green, "Damn, now we'll have them! See what you can do for Lieutenant Sutherland."

Lieutenant Moreau saluted back. Scanned the green but could not pick Lieutenant Sutherland from the mass of red. Easier to direct his attention at a motley gaggle of brown and dun homespun gathered like brown sheep milling across the commons.

Rebels.

This grungy group no more organized than a pail of porridge.

The colonial in charge, he knew from dispatches, was Captain Parker. And Moreau found the man rather easily, as Parker was older, and yet shouting at the top of his lungs, barely made a noise. Consumption was eating the rebel officer up from the inside and Parker's voice could barely raise above a whisper. If anyone heard the man, you couldn't tell. But the dunclads seemed to be trying to pay attention to their officer – yet still milled confusedly about, never quite falling in line.

Then at once the rebel Parker steadily grew in stature and authority; a shaft of light from the rising sun lanced across the green and Moreau could see his broad gestures, a strong wave of the arm, another fierce finger pointing at an open space of ground. And as if by magic, the mass of dunclads began to form themselves into some kind of parade-ground formation. In full plain sight they suddenly became an orderly mass of men, not lurking behind walls or hovering in open windows. But standing up like real soldiers, alert, organized, and spoiling for a fight.

Musket barrels glinted in that lance of sunlight but seemed perfectly harmless. In fact, the whole scene felt perfectly harmless, almost comic. A confused rabble unable to gather itself into a fighting unit, suddenly coming together like good little toy soldiers while the mass of men in scarlet filled out into the clipped grass. Invincible and hard.

More and more of them. Dwarfing the dunclad block. Sturdy Royal regulars, soberly gathering in rows like they'd been trained. Lieutenant Moreau's own troops filing out into the sunlight on a chill April morn, quickly organizing themselves into a strong red line, without having to be told.

Across the green the confused sounds of homespun rebels made grunting noises like herd animals loosed from a pen; then faded to silence.

And the world seemed to hold its breath.

Rebel Captain Parker's voice rose over his lung disease, a massive effort to speak, and Moreau heard the words running over the greensward:

"Stand your ground. Stand. Do not fire. Do not fire unless fired upon. But if they mean to have a war, let it begin here."

Begin here? Had these provincials not been fighting in all but musket fire these last ten years? Damn me, Moreau thought – had this execrable affair not been going on and on since forever? Why else had they sailed a thousand miles over the ocean blue to this grimy dung-strewn town on the edge of the world?

Captain Parker's voice fainter now, strained out to whispers. Moreau couldn't hear the rebel's orders. Yet the provincial's trained band of outlaws, a sturdy block of men, kept filing out of the trees.

As for the redcoats, one block of regulars appeared, then another, then another. The obvious hopelessness of the rebel position became clearer and clearer by the moment. Then Captain Parker's voice drifted across the greensward. What was he doing? It sounded as if the officer was ordering his men to disband, withdraw in the face of royal forces.

Was Captain Parker truly oblivious that no matter what – whether his rebels be strong or weak – the mass of regulars in red had marched out a dozen miles and would not return without the capture of a rebel leader? Or the securing of contraband? Or the sharp bark of Brown Bess spilling blood on the field this day?

As for Moreau, the idea of retreat before an overwhelmed, feeble rebel force with no musket unfired, the height of folly. The rebels had no choice. Disband, withdraw, melt away. For clearly, the King's men had come to settle business. The business of who owned what – the business of who owned whom. The business of who told who – how it was – and what was what. As the Yankee Doodle song said:

Yankee Doodle came to town,
For to buy a firelock,
We will tar and feather him,
And so we will John Hancock

And finding neither Hancock nor caches of arms, nor barns full of supplies, nor hoards of rebel firearms and firelocks – all that remained was a bitter taste of time and energy. As though to sheathe the blade without it tasting blood – a desecration of the uniform, a tacit admission that these rag-tags had bested the finest military in the world, made them dance to the lyrics of a rebel tune in a dark rude place of taunting, drunken sods. Now laughing at them to their faces across the commons, after a night's march in sodden boots.

Yet, looking at the wavering block of men across the way the Lieutenant could not imagine under what circumstances, the croaking Captain Parker might deign to bring his own trained guard troops into action. For some reason, the harried, tubercular voice of the Captain carried across the field, ordering his men, the exact opposite of what they'd already done. First Form. Now disband. Oddly, it made sense in its own way, the massive show of red was like some looming colossus erupting out of the trees encroaching the road. Daunting, intimidating, dwarfing all opposition:

"Disband now. We've done our point. Disband. Disperse. Back to your homes, back to your farms."

But God knows, it was too late for that.

You could tell by the way the King's Men organized there was no turning away. No slinking off from a fight. From his own position guarding the flanks of the regiment, Moreau saw another troop of Marines, an advanced guard out ahead of them. The new Marine troop stepped smartly into the greensward, flanking the mass of uniformed men coming up behind like a ribbon of scarlet. When the full contingent appeared off the road and formed up in the commons, the Marine detachment and Pitcairn's men would dwarf the provincials.

In a few short moments, the King's men organized themselves, the front rows falling to one knee, the muskets pointing as one. A daunting, overwhelming show of force. Now the rebel band of eighty fools looked even more hopelessly outmatched.

In a flash, Moreau saw the outcome in his head before a single shot was fired.

A massacre.

A slew of dunclad bodies dropping like flies to musket fire, the fleeing rustics scattering like maggots in the sun.

"This is stupid," he whispered to himself.

Did he actually say it out loud? Yes, out loud.

Neither sergeant nor corporal needed to be told twice. Yes, this action was stupid in every respect. Strong red lines of men against a gelatinous mob of disorganized rabble. The rabble stood for a few moments, stoically, hopelessly, then quietly withered, as the mass of redcoats showed no sign of mercy.

Sgt. Bates immediately grasped the crux of it, "Yes sir, very stupid. Only problematic if they run away. Otherwise, we'll see a good bloody morning."

A pointed glance at Sgt. Bates and Cpl. Cummins confirmed as much. He added a sharp glare and a sharper nod, "Well then! Let's get on with it".

"Stupid," Cpl. Cummins repeated to no one in particular, echoing the common thought. Lieutenant Moreau mounted the Good Belle and joined his troop along the line. Talking again to himself, but loudly enough for his officers to hear:

"Remember Gentlemen, "The wasp can't kill you, but unlike the good hardworking colonial honeybee, the American wasp can sting you even after it is crushed."

From where he sat, mounted on Good Belle, Lieutenant Moreau could plainly see the entire green. For a few moments he held the reins and silently stroked her shoulder. The Provincials milled about after their momentary military assembly, with more arriving every moment.

Once told to disband, the rustics searched in vain for some kind of order.

Another red-coated officer, another Lieutenant rode toward the mess of dunclads waving an unsheathed sword and shouting something on the order of, "Lay down your arms, drop your firearms, surrender your firelocks!"

Even the rebel leader wanted it over. Captain Parker strode back and forth, waving his sword and calling out hoarsely to his own men, "Go home! Go home!"

But it was all too late. The sword unsheathed yearns for blood. The noise all around seemed to rise like a wave, orders and rumbles from the red-coated throngs, and another roar of anger from the now two or three hundred simmering rebels in the field.

Faint echoes, of "go home…it's over…go home…" amongst some in the mob. But to no avail. The voices of caution drowned out in a swell of focused fury. Out of many – One. Even disorganized, uncouth and directionless, the rebel militia clung to their weapons and shouted abuse.

A stuttering mess of untucked shirts, frock coats, limp hose and gun barrels – one man tripping over his buckled shoes, falling into another who fell into another like tenpins, then struggling to rise again and gain their footing. Musket butts clattering, the cold steel barrels occasionally flashing in the morning light.

Did someone shout to disperse again?

Yes. British Major Pitcairn on horseback, shouting, "Disperse, you fools!" with pistol outstretched. But as he wore a redcoat with epaulettes of flashing gold, no dunclad paid him the slightest mind, instead laughing as he pranced back and forth on horseback like a popinjay, waving his silly pistol. A kindly man, with as kind a face as any lamb, and big doe eyes, he cut no terrifying figure, more like a porcelain doll in uniform. An object of ridicule more than fear.

Lieutenant Moreau heard the shot, before he saw anyone fall. Good Belle shifted nervously beneath him and he stroked her back to sensibility. The popinjay Major's horse threatened to rear and bolt, but quickly calmed. Lieutenant Moreau couldn't tell if the shot came from the dunclad fools or the strong red line.

Then he saw a British soldier in the mass of red slowly keel over. The soldier shivered as though touched by God, then fell to his knees.

Obviously shot, but from where?

The soldier rose with a limp arm, clearly wounded by some rebel, but not from the gathered mob. Cowardly shot from behind a wall or from the window of a building? From a place of concealment, behind a hedge? No way to tell.

On his own side, behind the redcoat, Lieutenant Moreau noticed a rebel prisoner, back of the red line, suddenly break free and sprint off like a jackrabbit. A redcoat gave chase, then realizing he'd never catch the man, discharged his Brown Bess to stop the escaped prisoner. As the rebel leapt a low wall the musket ball caught him in the back and he disappeared behind it.

Seeing this sent a shiver of savagery through the ranks. A wildness overtook everyone. Every redcoat infected with an unrestrained thrill. A shivering current running through the King's men like an electric St. Vitus' Dance. Lieutenant Moreau saw his men ready to slash and pulverize every stinking colonist at the first twitch of dunclad fire and steel.

Then suddenly – with no warning – a dozen British ranks fired as one. A wave of smoke and thunder engulfed the green. But no rebels fell – they must have fired nothing but powder. Powder without ball. A useful enough tactic to scare and intimidate without doing any real harm. Noisy as hell and almost as effective as laying down a barrage of fully loaded muskets.

A warning shot.

But to no avail.

Totally ignored.

If the rebel Captain Parker ever countermanded that final command for the militia to disperse – or ordered instead to attack – Prepare your firearms, aim your firearms! Those orders were lost in the noise and confusion of the minute. The hour of decision never to be undone.

The mass of colonials meandered about like lost, demented things. Some stood in one place, while others adhered to their formation. Some even seemed to shiver, cowering off to the shadows of the trees or behind stone walls.

Somehow it was mysteriously decided to disarm the rebels. The stupidest idea so far. Major Pitcairn lifted his sword, so it caught the light and pointed at the amorphous mass across the green. Moreau knew a worse order could not have been conceived in heaven or hell.

All winter the dirty, smelly locals had taunted every King's Man like it was their personal business. Rocks in snowballs, then ice balls, then frozen horse dung. The bad food, the slop buckets dumped on every barracks doorstep – it had built and built and now an officer of the King pointed with his saber at the very despicable human crud responsible for months of abuse.

The King's Men needed no further encouragement. Bayonets fixed, glinting like bristles from a porcupine, the troops closest to Major Pitcairn shouted as one, and instead of marching stoically across the sward, took off at a trot, bayonets levelled at any fool dumb enough stand in the way. Facing the charge, one or two of the dunclads opened fire. Turning the onslaught of red-coated men from joyous anger to righteous rage.

The soldiers' trot turned to a charge.

Which is when Humpty Dumpty fell from the wall.

Charging regulars, scattering locals, some turning to discharge their own weapons even as they fled. Another nearby well-formed Lobster company prepared, aimed and fired. A murderous volley.

The smoke of discharge, one after another seemed to fill the green. That was enough for the King's men. All at once the entire green engulfed in gunfire. Major Pitcairn's strong red line discharged like one single broadside, without even a command. A dozen dunclads fell amongst themselves. Scattered, skittering off behind houses, and into nearby gardens and woods.

So, all the King's horses and all the King's men – four-score men and four-score more – slaughtered Humpty Dumpty where he fell.

Villagers lay on the ground. Moreau couldn't count how many – too much smoke. But enough to call the exchange a rout. No sign of the rebel Captain

Parker, no sign of further resistance, no point in racing through the woods in search of armed dunclads, scampering off like rabbits. They'd never catch enough to make the chase worthwhile.

Lt Moreau was about to order his men to help the wounded, when Major Pitcairn, called out, "That's enough now, gentlemen – they'll be here when we return." And flashed his sword in the direction of Concord.

He meant these despicable rustics. The fallen villagers on the green. Only one British soldier had been wounded in the arm – though whether by musket ball or bayonet Moreau couldn't say. Some officer gave the man leave to limp back to Boston on the shoulder of another.

The sound of men's groans filled the air as the less bloody dragged the bloodier off the small battlefield. Windows were raised and doors thrown open in every house facing the green, accepting all who could gain entry. In a few moments the wounded disappeared inside houses and parlors. As for the provincial dead left where they fell, Moreau quickly counted seven or eight bodies lying on the grass, not moving. For the moment, no one came for them.

The remaining King's soldiers under Major Pitcairn grew increasingly restive, and confused, as to their mission and purpose. A few had reloaded and began firing at the houses, breaking windows and leaving burning shot in doors and lintels.

In a hopeless attempt to restore order, the Major shouted an order to his drummer. "Beat Assembly!"

And the drummer, now with a job to do, beat assembly mercilessly until the pulse of it drowned out every other thought or intention and the men came together. Mayhem turned to regimentation, the soldiers on the green steadily came to order. An odd quiet returned to the green, like invisible curtains in the air. And Major Pitcairn's soft orders went to lieutenants and thence to sergeants – and it became clear what was wanted. Muskets loaded with powder, the troops in a row.

Now a victory volley, shot off into the air as one, like an exclamation point at the end of a sentence! Echoing off into the trees, bouncing off the houses and quietly drifting off down the roads.

Yet a sour taste remained in Moreau's mouth.

And he felt the urge to spit.

Moreau nodded to his men, "Let us go, Gentlemen."

Then drily, to Sergeant Bates and Corporal Cummins, "Concord's waiting on us. Let's see if it's still there. We can't let it run off."

Chapter Fifteen: The Bridge

Concord

As the sun climbed, the night's march and the day's exertions took a greater toll. The men were drained, thirsty and hungry. Lieutenant Moreau looked about for a friendly or willing tavern, even a stream to rest and bivouac. But found nothing suitable. His troop crossed no stream, no brook, and the muddy puddles along the march were fetid or cracked. But not too early for Spring's gnats. A yellow ugly rime seemed to infect each damp swale, with a cloud of hovering no-see-ums.

But orders were orders. Move west. Immediately.

Yet they'd found no goods or stores in any house, barn or shed.

Lieutenant Moreau expected nothing less. Their noisy advance from Boston a banging parade. Military achievement so far – the torn bits of incompetent homespun rebellion laying on the Lexington Green.

Bloody grass.

Hollow victory.

Still, Lieutenant Moreau marched his men outward, ever westward. A bend in the road of a fallow field with a broken length of stone wall beckoned him. Open but dry. A quarter mile away, a stone bridge leapt a small stream. This is where they headed and in a few more minutes his men went down for water. A place of respite.

"We'll take a quarter-hour now," he told Bates and Cummings.

How little did he know that fifteen minutes would be the last moment of blessed relief for the worst day of their lives. In another two hours, it would be march or die.

Fight or die –

But how could he know? He should have known.

The rebels' clamor had spread far and wide. He knew that much. He knew it in his guts. Not his bowels, not the loose, impending urgency of a bad oyster – but in his guts, a clenched fist, higher up, "The Colonel's Thumb" he called it. The grasping fingers of a brutal, faceless officer, reaching up into his chest to hold his heart and lungs for ransom.

This breather, this bivouac by the stone wall, galvanized him like an electrostatic current. Every little thing touched him with a needle of understanding:

– the glitter of dew on blades of grass, great goblets of water for mice and grasshoppers.

– a collapsed hay rig in the midst of the fallow field, flattened by rain and snow. Fallen hay brought into the burrows of every rabbit, fox and mole to warm and cushion their nest and bolt holes.

Then Meg's face came to him unbidden. Staring at him as though from an artist's sketch paper. He'd seen an ochre charcoal by Watteau once, *Seated Woman*, one hand covering her clothed breast, in fetching modesty. The subject's attitude, neither frightened nor surprised, but open to the attentions of some admirer.

And Meg could have been his model. In Moreau's mind, Meg wore the white chemise and bodice of a milkmaid. The costume, oddly appropriate. A wisp of golden straw clung to her hair as though she had just come from the gleaning of the fields. The vision faded. The stone wall and clammy Massachusetts returned, chilling his thighs.

Down below, as his men went down to drink, the Lieutenant worried a single strand of straw between thumb and forefinger like a Greek fisherman with his worry beads. Would dear Meg have ever done the same with some trinket while thinking of him? Hold something between thumb and forefinger and speak his name …?

He doubted it. Deflated. His breath stale inside.

And that was enough to get him off the stone wall, barking to Sergeant Bates and Corporal Cummins:

"That'll do. Let's get on with it."

Everyone could hear and see the rebels retreating out of Lexington. At first disorderly, then in more order as they came together. A tramping mass pushing on towards Concord. Moreau knew there'd be more Royal compatriots waiting for them there, and more replacements after the rebels arrived. This was less a rout than a strategic retreat from which the local peasantry could mount another blockheaded defense.

In less than an hour, his soldiers reached Concord proper. The column of red moved into the town in scattered twos and threes, not like a scarlet tide, but scattershot.

By the time Moreau's men arrived behind the main column the previous troops had fanned out into the town, flanking the road. The first group of soldiery, still pursuing rebels, entered buildings to secure firing positions for all who passed below. At least in this way the sharp eyes in windows overlooking the road were friendly eyes and the glint of weapons friendly weapons.

Other companies fanned out to search for contraband. And there was a great noise of confiscations, mayhem and breakage as King's men turned houses inside out, trampled kitchen gardens and searched for loot. The shrieks of goodwives protesting the theft and seizure of every household item echoed from one house to another all along the street. Soldiers emerged with what they could carry, a coffee grinder, a rope of garlic, half a dozen eggs in a net, wads of sheet music, a clutch of smoking pipes in a felt bag.

Pointless vandalism that did nothing to advance the King's prerogatives.

Buried cannons were found in a field, too massive to move or transport, instead they burned trunnions and gun carriages and carriage wheels. Anything that rolled or moved. Now the cannons were useless.

Barrels of salted beef and flour dumped in a millpond. A house caught on fire by accident and Moreau ordered his men to assist with the bucket brigade.

Then came the bridge.

A narrow span of no account. The small river could be forded by canoe over a dozen paddle strokes. A sluggish grass-grown waterway, thick with reeds and sedges growing without too much trouble from muddy banks. But this damp April morning, the river was swollen from Spring floodwaters, a formidable moat of brown ugly water rushing to the sea.

Boats or no boats, there'd be no crossing other than the bridge.

The rebels had already retreated off the span and seemed intent on making a stand at the road and adjacent fields by the far end. But their gathered ranks looked more like a mass of confusion. Nothing in order, just armed men, two or three hundred or so milling about, directionless. A Protean mass of muskets.

Whereas Moreau watched his men on the column approach in slightly better ranks and form. A deep red, tramping column at easy march. Without the urgency of imminent hostilities. While a handful of other redcoat regulars, posted at the crossing retreated off the bridge in a disorderly gang. Half a dozen men in scarlet confusion – never a welcome sign.

The first troop to reach the span paused at the bridge entrance and dropped to their knees. Firearms shouldered and locked in place, with barely an order given. The other chaotic redcoats found their nerve and joined the others, shouldering their firearms.

At the call of an officer a flanking movement ordered to protect those on the road proper. But few if any King's men broke from the main troop of firing lines.

Nevertheless, professional soldiery against an angry mob. (Facing off on the far side of the stream?) An imminent slaughter. The colonials had no chance. No chance.

But before Moreau's own men could even join the confused formation the rebels massed and formed a loose firing block. Rebel leaders begged restraint. Faint orders from the far side of the span drifted into the air. Hold your fire, hold your fire! Hold – !

Suddenly by God's comic grace, the ridiculous figure of a man appeared. A non-combatant emerging into the fields of fire. Clearly disturbed, the madman was dressed in a ragged waistcoat, breeches and buckled shoes. The ragamuffin held a huge jug and a clutch of worn, cracked mugs. Going from man to man, apparently, the odd fellow was offering to sell hard cider to anyone who wanted to wet their whistle. Hurriedly he was shooed away. "To the madhouse with you! Bugger off!" came the calls, and some much worse.

While middle of the bridge, some of the King's soldiers were clumsily trying to yank loose planks from the span, tearing them up and tossing them into the water. Obviously, to stop the rebel advance, to stop the colonials from crossing the river.

Until another officer shouted at them to leave off.

No destroying the King's bridge. Especially not with a handful of Redcoats still on the far side.

And by this time the mass of rebels had gelled into a shivering pudding, the muskets came up all at once, but no one fired. Awaiting orders?

What orders? No one knew.

A redcoat opened fire with a single shot. Nerves? Again, who knew?

But one rebel went down, wounded.

More men in the red ranks replied in kind. More random shots. With no one in command. Across the span the militia had become a sullen angry mob. Another sporadic, feeble volley from the King's men. More colonials fell. And finally rebel orders changed, some Colonial shouting, "Fire, you fools! Fire!" And all at once the command was obeyed.

The rebels fired as one. A huge single boom, and more smoke and more shrieks of fear and pain. Four redcoat officers fell and nearly a score of privates. A real blooding now. One lieutenant was shot in the face, through his cheeks, leaving a ragged crimson mouth flap that could be seen from every angle. And Moreau could feel the men at his back bristle with anger. Dogs of war straining at the leash. But terrified as well, anger and fear mixed together.

Worse still, the King's command was a faltering mess.

A half dozen redcoats at the entrance of the bridge and either side of the road lay on the ground, wounded or dead. They'd gone down like tenpins to shrieks of fear and dismay.

Then as powder smoke drifted through the ranks no one could see the hand before their face. Then the smoke cleared in the dead air. A mass of redcoats lay on the grass sward along the near riverbank. So many you couldn't see the earth beneath them. A wanton, disgraceful slaughter. All the more shameful that it had to happen at all.

The mass of King's men now scattered – their resolution simply wiped out in a single volley. Leaving nothing behind but the acrid stink of powder and ball and a grotesque silence, punctuated by final sounds of dying men.

Outnumbered and confused, the King's soldiers retreated from the bridge in a ragged mass. Abandoned men lay on the ground. And Moreau ordered his own to drag or carry the wounded to safety on a nearby hill.

This proved ineffective at best, as many more rebels reinforced their numbers across the river. And Moreau's men suddenly abandoned following orders altogether, melting away from the enemy even as fresh redcoats, reinforcements came up from town. Those, his wavering men saw and gravitated to the replacements as if the Almighty come to save them.

Safety in numbers.

For a fleeting moment, Moreau weighed this rebel victory in the grand scale of things. A skirmish well-executed by amateurs in the face of disorganized professionals.

The King's men lay where they fell, some moving weakly, others never to move again. And seeing the dead and dying like that, Moreau felt a brief wave of doubt. One of their men looked like he'd been scalped, and whether true or not made no difference.

There was no call for this.

Like a missing fork at a silverware table setting, like a broken shoelace, like horse dung splattered up from the muck onto your coat collar. All things that challenged and darkened the heart.

But with a supreme act of will, the Lieutenant put such thoughts aside. The King's soldiery was the toughest, greatest force on earth. To join the mass of red was like assembling in a great fortress on a mountaintop. Inviolate, massive and secure. No one could ever drive against them and survive.

Yet there was no disputing the King's men had fumbled the opening shot in this grim business. No one could argue with that. Even the provincials across the river seemed astonished at their success. A sort of happy stunned pause, filled with mumbles of expectation and surprise. Well done, lads, well done.

Expect no more. Round one to rebels, but the day was young.

So, if the Lieutenant knew anything, he knew the King's men would own the battleground ere long. And the rebels crushed in due course.

Part II

Chapter Sixteen: House of Dead Eyes

Strategic Withdrawal
Noon Onwards
A Narrow Road to Boston

Instead of an immediate return to Boston, a general halt had been called in the town of Concord where there were still supplies to find, doors to break down, and windows to smash. The King's men took their time over lunch, stealing what they could from homestead, farm, cottage, barn or tavern. And when fully rested, gathered themselves in an orderly fashion – prepared to return to Boston and barracks.

The hostiles for their part lost no time reinforcing their positions and ranks all along the line from Concord back to Lexington. Moreau could feel them in his bowels. The awful urge to let loose with nothing behind it.

A few rebels appeared here and there, then vanished back into the trees. And Moreau didn't like the look of that either. The appearance of a few men scattered about hid the fact that hundreds more lay in wait, unseen. Rebels massing in nearby fields and furrows, while the King's own men dawdled and laughed away the noontime repast. Then finally finishing lunch, brushing themselves off, slinging the straps on their packs and guns and shuffling into a column.

Would you call it a retreat or a return?

A return. The troops were in good order, the men in good spirits. And they all knew the distance back. Knowing how far you must go allows a man to measure his resources against the distance and the struggle. It's not knowing that kills a man.

And the disappointment in their failure to find supplies or leaders worth arresting didn't seem to have affected anyone one way or the other. A good thing only one wounded and limping back to barracks – so all was right with the world. You could hear the high spirits in their voices, and bits of jokes and bits of laughter, and half told stories –

"No nappies for you – "

"The balloonist promised to marry them – "

"The scones were free with the purchase of a petticoat – "

Such was the tenor of things said, heard or ignored on the road back to Boston. First marching in general order but little by little becoming an undulating snake as the Lobsters retreated.

At first, Command sensibly ordered a flanking party to guard their retreat. The flanking party found a ridge overlooking the line of return. Redcoat muskets kept the large party of colonials following them at a safe distance. This would work for about a mile, but almost at once a narrow bridge appeared jumping a narrow stream.

Up till now the colonial militia had only been making threatening noises, haphazardly firing, out of range. Keeping safe distance from the flanking units, more of an angry rabble than a military force. But as the mass of King's men approached this bridge, it coalesced into an irritated herd. The regulars converged, consolidated, in an exasperated red mob for their turn across.

The bridge could only accommodate three men abreast, the chokepoint puddling the King's soldiers like red sludge in a stopped drain. And this traffic jam invited the first of many attacks. Moreau watched in growing dismay as colonials wasted no time in addressing this vulnerability. More militia companies appeared from out of nowhere, the north and the east, too many to count. Massing together, the hostiles didn't even wait for an order to fire but advanced to musket range.

With a surge of relief Moreau's troop crossed the bridge, shuffling through three abreast – and from the far bank watched as the King's rear guard let fly a volley.

Finally in range the massed rebels returned fire. Two more regulars fell and did not get up while half a dozen redcoats writhed, wounded on the ground.

From what Moreau and every other Brit could see –

No rebels fell whatsoever.

And it was this King's Officer's, this redcoat's first inkling this day was about to take a turn for the ugly.

Matters went from unfortunate to brutal in barely an hour. Moreau almost lost sight of his men, as their uniforms blended into the long red column. The road then followed the base of a broad hill. A very vulnerable field position. The crest above a fine firing point for anyone forced to march below.

At first, seeing the heights free of all hostile guns, their hearts lightened. The Lieutenant – competent mapmaker that he was – recalled this bluff was called Hardy's Hill. Then recalled some locals called it Brooks Hill, and why the hill possessed two names instead of just one, mystified him this morning as it had on that winter's mapmaking. And as the redcoat column came under this hill's gaze – it became horribly clear the provincials indeed held the high ground.

Hundreds of militia men suddenly appeared above looking down, and this time, not as a rabble but forming a competent, well-ordered force. In a flash of command imbecility, the lead redcoats were ordered to take the hill.

No, not pause –

Not regroup on more favorable ground, or find a better redoubt. Nor lure the hostiles into a favorable firing point of British choosing –

No –

Instead, Command ordered a frontal charge up the hill. Multiple companies started first at a high step, then slowly growing to a run, packs and cartridge belts clanking out the tempo of attack. Moreau's men fell in last and so he could see everything up ahead. White breeches stumping up and down like pistons, black boots trampling the grass, muskets held at high port. The growing rumble of a charge – the hundred angry throats.

But in the face of attack the rebels held firm. They drew down as one and muskets fired, a monstrous thunderclap in every ear and a tidal wave of gun smoke. In the space of a moment, Moreau found himself standing among the groaning and the dead on the side of a hill, in a fog of sulfur.

Their attack had been completely repulsed. A score of British soldiery lay on the slope of the hill. Sergeant Bates and Corporal Cummins stood among the grisly wounded of the front company and both men looked at him with the strangest expression on their white faces.

What now? Keep on or retreat?

While the rebels not fifty yards above, methodically reloaded their firearms. Nothing to do but retreat. No point in struggling up the slope again in the teeth of powder and shot. Numbing fear seemed to course through their veins, not blood.

Fear? Already?

Who cared? Not Moreau. Any advance up the hill came to a swift end. Without even the slightest protest, he was swept down the hill with the rest, half run, half stumble. Yet he had the opportunity to study the faces retreating beside him. Faces clodhopping along, not in panic or fear – but simple sad faces in a state of stoic confusion. Grim faces sending the simplest message. Find another spot. Let's find another spot.

At the base of the slope the curve of the road bent into a lightly wooded bit of forest. An empty cathedral of trees. A few of the wounded were dragged down the hill, crying out as each bump hit some gash or bone break. Then laid out against this tree or that to wait for aid.

Moreau could see one or two more wounded still on the hill, feebly moving. But one look at Sergeant Bates' and Corporal Cummins' drawn faces scotched the idea of ordering them up the slope again. Better to find another spot from which to fight. Besides, the forward companies were moving on down the road, and faint orders to resume march drifted back at them.

Before they'd stumped on half a mile, the troops bumped shoulders again at yet another bridge crossing. A line of rebels was waiting to let fly a volley. A grim brown and green line in the woods like a row of hedges.

A glance told Moreau all he needed to know. Provincials in prone position or kneeling behind boulders or crouched in thickets, their musket barrels sighted in at the men like the bristle of a porcupine. Each barb ready to sting.

More firing again, more wounded – but the regulars pushed across and kept going. Moreau barely looked left or right off his path, so eager was he to move his men back across the span. They tromped over the bridge at a hard trot, that clean bit of open road ahead beckoning them onward.

The road rose, a rocky field coming into sight. At first Moreau saw nothing, as rebel militia wore the brown and dun homespun. But as they reached this rocky field, it became all too clear how many militia men there were. The militiamen, a sort of undulating crawling fungus crouching behind fallen trees and quietly watching from boulder to boulder. More than enough to harry and wound his men.

On both sides of the road, the dun and brown homespun swelled in numbers, while those they had hoped to outrun and leave behind now reached firing range. Three sides covered. The redcoat column writhed again and more men fell at the random fire. Bullets flew at them like wasp stings from every direction along the line of retreat. The pace quickened, as if to get out of this trap. Another 500 yards at quick march. Another curve in the road, another volley from militia positioned on either side of the road.

How many fell this time? Moreau lost count. Several score at least.

The quick march turned into a run. On either side, thicker woods and spotty swamps kept the rebels stuck and yet that deadly growing fungus could not gel to any decent size. In desperation the colonials formed a roiling mob, too close together on the road, too packed, falling over themselves in their stupid haste to get at the King's men. Random fire at best, and no time to pause and reload. The militiamen couldn't mass again, many turned to stragglers, falling and tripping in the swamps and wetting their breeches and firelocks.

Undisciplined chaos behind gave the King's men a moment's respite.

But not to last.

On every side a swelling tide seemed to rise, that dun clad, homespun mass growing like a tumor in one's guts. Pretty orchards, in spring leaf on either side, perfect ground for men to mass before firing on the road and the slithering red serpent. The numbers of hostiles grew and grew, more than a thousand now, then two thousand, a mass of men that could not be counted by eye, but felt like whirlpool sucking you into its maw.

Yes, Command sent more flanking parties out, waiting till the dun clads passed then firing at their rear. But for every musket fired, another had to return fire and in retreat the red serpent spent more powder and ball out of range than on the mark. While militiamen harried the column, struck again and again, wounding some, killing some, and redcoat bodies lay behind the retreat like a trail of blood.

Moreau had given up ordering his men to do anything but move fast, keep up. And as things became dicey, angry rats and nasty badgers came out of the underbrush to nip and snap at every soldier's ankles. Behind every tree, the mongoose made the snake turn to fight, another pair of snapping jaws bared, another set of snapping teeth, sinking a fang into the serpent's shanks –

Writhe and snap, twitch and shiver, drops of blood.

Skirmish by skirmish.

Leaving the serpent, a twitching wounded mess.

But before the mass of men cleared the next turn, a rebel picket line appeared like ghosts on the brown crest of winter's grass along the rise. Some among the rebels could be seen limping into position, some with white bandages on their arms or legs, where they were wounded in the previous exchange.

What grit, Moreau thought. A sinking admiration grew in him. Expanding through him like lightning through a rod. These rubes were more than mortal men, but stele stones of ancient gods, stuck in place for eons. Not to be trifled with, not to be moved, but best left alone to the wind and the stars.

Command had made a deep mistake coming out from safe Boston, coming out from the smoky taverns and the warm barracks. Better to have stayed in bed that day. Played cards. Gotten drunk. Better to have simply turned the other cheek. Never crossed the cold Charles River. Or sailed to these hostile shores.

And as if to make the point – how uncommonly resilient these rebels were, so no one on this earth, neither enlisted Regular, nor white-wigged British officer could ever misunderstand again – another volley erupted from the uphill picket line. Fire from above, a dun clad homespun gaggle standing or kneeling in a ragged line. One ball found its lucky way to an officer astride a horse.

A Major or a Colonel? Moreau couldn't tell at this distance. But he saw the gold braid and epaulets shiver, the tricornered hat fly off as the man took a ball to the chest. The officer seemed to hover for a moment on his mount, then keel over like a toy soldier. While his horse bolted off across a field with a ghost for a rider.

Still, Command would not relent or take the hint that these men were not to be trifled with. That this day's engagement would not go as planned. No rethinking the proposition.

Despite the obvious and sensible option to regroup or God forbid, retreat – Command once again ordered two companies to brave the fire and take the hill, as if doing the same thing all over again would achieve a different result.

This second assault didn't make it halfway, not fifty yards. Another volley rained down and a line of redcoats staggered to their knees en masse. But worse than that, if there could be such a thing, a thing worse than regulars going down, oh yes there could – one hot lead ball found the gold braid and epaulets – a second officer was struck.

Now both officers of Boston Command were laid low. Though this one, this time just injured, the officer knocked from his horse and writhing on the ground. Yet wounded like this seemed somehow worse than outright killed – the silent groans and twitching about like an injured sparrow. And worse because the regulars finally saw their leaders as frail and human and broken on the field.

Then there was the exhaustion of every man jack out there that mid-morning. The Lieutenant could feel it for them, through every fiber of his being. They were tired. All of them. Tired. And thirsty again. The lust for water, for any drink swelling their throats closed, their lips cracking. And even if they weren't in such a miserable state, there was something even worse – they were near out of ammunition. Powder, wadding, ball all seemed to have vanished in the few exchanges since their march out. The emptiness of frock pockets in every lad. A kind of hopelessness spreading from man to man, from a few men to the whole group.

And then Moreau saw the unthinkable. Two men, then three – split off from the regulars, dropping their muskets and approaching whatever formed the rebel lines, hands outstretched. The weak, weeping figures of surrender.

And whether because there was no senior officer to lead them or because Moreau knew no one would pay attention to his command, whether there was some unspoken agreement throughout the ranks or mere gut cowardice – the question – fight or flight – resolved itself in a hair's breadth. One man ran, and then another, and then –

The whole group. Hammering down the road as if the devil were after them.

Lieutenant Moreau in the rushing current attempted some kind of command, a shout of, "Form Ranks!" from the saddle. But gave up when his voice barely reached his own ears. Better to dismount and save the horse. No one else could hear him either and he found himself sprinting like a rabbit along with everyone else, leading Belle by the halter. The rushing current of men drew them on like rapids on a river.

He could feel the men about him flagging as they ran. And he knew in his guts the whole group was ready to throw down their arms, raise their hands and surrender.

But as if to forestall the inevitable humiliation – yet another sound came from further on. A rumble of voices growing to a beastly roar from the cluster of houses on the edge of Lexington.

The unmistakable sound of men shouting in assurance. No –

Cheering.

A full brigade. A thousand men had marched out to rescue them. The redcoats gathered in the main thoroughfare, as though bursting out the seams of the town. The rebels fired from various positions off the main. But no one fell. Bad aim all around.

More importantly two Royal cannons were pushed to the front. The two field pieces hastily brought into position, loaded – and before the Lieutenant could take a breath the cannon fired two salvos at the gathering rabble. The gaggle of clods froze in their tracks, as the hot projectiles sailed into the trees.

Rebels turned to rude, rustic statues.

Stunned in every manner of awkward pose.

If the King's men loaded grapeshot and fired again, they'd go down like tenpins.

Sensing its imminent doom, the mob pulled away, back into trees and behind shrubs and stone walls. At first a wave of relief like cool water flowed through Moreau. Then he grasped with all grit and sand the militia's tactics. They would not stand still for a fight. They would not gather into a formation. They would harry and tarry, they would pursue and cover, they would take their time reloading, picking targets, and flit about like vicious insects, stinging and darting away. This was how it was to be.

And no one on earth could change that.

No one in Command, no regular, no officer, commissioned or otherwise. The American wasp was going to sting them to death, bit by bit, step by step, mile by mile all the way to Boston.

Chase the rebels into field or copse and they would scatter.

Let them run off, dissolve – evaporate – and at the next turn, the next straightaway, the next narrow lane, the stinging wasps would appear again. A swarm of musket fire engulfing whatever bit of the red serpent was exposed. And red blood would seep blackly through red coats and red virulent patches through white britches.

Lieutenant Moreau writhed inside – finally grasping that the only thing the King's men, and marines of His Majesty's Colonial army managed to achieve was falling into a gorse bush face first. Then upon rising, struggling from the nettles.

Compounding injury, the British Army had stupidly stabbed a wasp's nest, stuck it on a pike, and waved it around. Releasing a thousand, winged stinging devils. To be stung and stung and stung again. Stung until they were poisoned with venom and lay with bloated faces unrecognizable to anyone but God.

The King's reinforcements enveloped the column and Moreau's men. They needed rest more than they could've ever known. This single pause in their flight let them feel the absolute depth of exhaustion and dread for all time, until the slow crawl back from the pit. The Lieutenant watched as his men found a seat, found a tree to lay against or simply collapsed on the ground, stretched out in exhaustion. Finding a welcoming bunk on any patch of grass.

Moreau found a flat sawed tree stump like a low stool and sat heavily. Belle strayed upon the grass to graze. Calm and aloof the horse showed a bleeding wound where a bullet had glanced along her rump, leaving a streak of burnt and shaved flesh.

An equine dueling scar.

And for a moment Moreau's ear tingled and burned in sympathy. A dueling scar of his own, long healed. The mark left by a saber blade, his ear, split and partially missing. The foolish Meg had almost got him killed. Maidens and misunderstandings were such a deadly combination.

"She'd known any number at the Hostings House!" the braggard said. Some other officer, a fool and coward to boot. "I don't remember her name, Marjorie, Merry, Margaret – a trollop if there ever was one."

Lieutenant Moreau stared coldly across the rude table of the tavern.

"Surely not Meg."

"Damn me, if it wasn't!" the officer said.

The fool, another lieutenant – grinned from ear to ear and Moreau vividly saw his saber splitting that grinning ape's face right through his wig.

"Surely you remember incorrectly."

Giving the witless fool more than ample opportunity to recollect differently.

"No, I remember quite well."

This man was a species of idiot. Walking into the duel with both eyes open.

"Then we shall have to reconfigure your memory for you, Sir."

But the fool was a better swordsman than a raconteur. And it was going badly for Moreau, the officer seeing his overall skill was superior, toyed with his lesser opponent. Looking to teach a crippling lesson rather than win a fight.

Taking his time, a nick here, a poke there, intent on taking one of Moreau's eyes. But the man seemed to trip on a bit of soft ground, lunging out of control and the saber sliced by the Lieutenant's head.

The better swordsman brought up short, impaled as he was – purely by accident – on his opponent's hovering blade. What Moreau remembered most clearly, the look of abject surprise on the man's face. And hearing his own mumbled reply, "I am sorry."

Then as the man burbled blood and slowly sank to the ground, "I should never have objected."

And then as if to seal the futility and stupidity of it all:

"It wasn't that important."

The look in the man's eyes that he might die for nothing stuck with Moreau when bloodier tableaus faded over time.

He was bitterly lucky that day. And his opponent as well. Six months to recover, a bowel infection that almost killed him. Somewhere along the line, Moreau heard the man had resigned his position and now ate and drank nothing but skim milk.

Meg's face returned to him again. The innocent milkmaid. A halo of soft light about her hair, the questioning doe eyes of a young deer. Worth a man's life? Who could say, men did stupid things for women, even for women they couldn't care less about. But what Moreau recalled most strongly from that moment in her family's garden was the softness of the air, the cherry trees in white and pink bloom, the blossoms starting to fall, and a gust of wind made a pink snowstorm across the orchard. Much like now, much like this moment.

For some reason Sgt. Bates took this exact moment to examine his Brown Bess, there was something on the firing pan and he quietly fussed over it as a man who fusses over a broken shoelace. The quiet of the moment seemed to imbue the very air with blessed peace and Moreau fell into a daydream, a quiet reverie of Meg and pink blossoms, of no particular consequence, when –

Out of nowhere, a gunshot broke the air.

Men jumped and looked about.

Except for Sgt. Bates. The Sergeant looked down at his chest, a broad bib of blood seeping to his belt.

"I'm shot," he murmured, somewhat surprised.

Corporal Cummins came to his side, even as his friend slumped sideways toward the ground. Nothing for it, but to watch helplessly as the sergeant died.

And after a moment, the man's heaving chest slowed, then stopped altogether.

Dead.

The knowledge of this casualty ran through the company like a pox – even with the men spread out across the orchard, scattered, under this tree or that. They saw Cummins cradling the body of Bates and knew the man was dead. You could see the same expression in every face, peeking from the trees, bushes or behind the stone walls – a pastiche of surprise, anger and fear. A man dead that could have been them.

A dead man they'd known since forever.

A man they trusted to stand by them. Now lifeless – realizing, as if for the first time – the dead cannot stand by you. There are no ghosts of warriors holding musket and the saber. No phantoms of the 300 standing in Thermopylae. No life from the fallen. No way back when a man walked that final path to the dark door at the end of the alley.

And that made this place, whatever its name, no longer safe. And somehow, Lieutenant Moreau had to pull his scattered men back into an organized column. A mass of men, not a scattered mourning mess.

With his last ounce of energy, the Lieutenant rose from his comfortable stump, and heard his voice carry farther and stronger than he had any reason to expect:

"Formation!"

The scattered faces looked now to him, not the fallen body of the sergeant:

"Formation! Ranks on me!"

Chapter Seventeen: March or Die

To Boston: March or Die

Exhaustion was the color of the day. Gasps over a bloated tongue. Tramping feet, every step forward, the road getting longer and longer in front of you – until the headlong rush became a stumbling rout in burning boots. At first Moreau tried to keep his men together, but stragglers were picked off, or fell behind – and it took the last remaining junior officer, Corporal Cummins, to keep the remaining men in good marching order.

Every time Moreau looked back there seemed to be fewer and fewer in the ranks, and greater gaps between the men who remained. They'd left Boston barracks with over 200 men, and now seemed to have 60 or less. This staggering loss of over half his troops crushed the very marrow of his bones. But Moreau dared not show it. And the most terrifying part – no one could tell by looking over their shoulder where the missing men had fallen. Scattered here or there, hidden in the trees or ditches or behind hedges – there was no organized effort to find those who lagged behind.

The cries and groans of the wounded seemed to follow them, hanging in the very air like bad smoke. Making Moreau's bravery shallow, flagging at best. He led the good Belle, trotting along on foot – demonstrating for every man jack that he would not ride off and flee. Showing the men in the thick of it, once and for all – that he was one of them.

And yet each mile brought another lash to the face, another stab in the ribs – stinging wasps flying in out of nowhere. Take their blood and bite of skin then vanishing into thin air.

The first tangle was a mere skirmish by a pond. Yet a bloody tangle, nonetheless.

In their headlong rush, Moreau's men crashed into another British column marching out from Boston. Command had sent out two additional ammunition wagons to supply the field pieces, a convoy to reinforce what had become headlong flight. Too late, futile, and now beside the point altogether.

When all at once, another group of rebels appeared out of nowhere along the nearest flanking hill. First an empty green ridge, spotted with a few trees, then suddenly darkened with a line of men. Even from a distance you could see these were older men, just by the way they walked and moved. Some struggled along a hillcrest as if needing a cane. Others stumbled, hesitant, catching their balance. While others were slow, uncertain, or frail. Clumsily ambling into position.

Yet despite their awkward puppet motions, the gray scarecrows formed a ragged line upon the overlooking rise and drew down on the convoy. Shouts from the hoarse throats above, clearly demanded surrender. "Lay down your arms! Surrender! Stand down!"

But surrender was not in the cards. No King's man took the orders of a rebel. Refusal was a King's man's only duty. Undeterred, unmoved – the soldiers ignored the rude ragamuffin noises along the ridge and pressed on. Red marching coats and wagon masters driving their noisy horses along the road below.

Defiant, and deaf to all entreaties.

Until the inevitable pok-pok-pok of gunfire fell like random darts amongst them. At first the redcoats thought the ragged firing missed their mark, as no one fell. But as the rebels found their targets, the fleeing redcoats began to shiver as they ran. For their targets were mostly horses, who now died in service to the King.

Soon a bloody, neighing mess on the road, along with two sergeants and some lieutenant who didn't make as much noise as wounded horses but thrashed about on the highway like a demented thing.

The remainder of the company, a half dozen or so, threw their weapons away in a nearby pond and raised their hands. You could see the odd splashing of the water as the pond swallowed one Brown Bess after another. Black water, confused ripples, muskets gone.

Moreau's troopers saw that breakaway group by the water surrender, and with a flash of strategic insight, the Lieutenant motioned to his men to make a wide circle into the trees, far from the ragged, defeated gaggle. Refusing to join those redcoats, Moreau's men avoided capture themselves.

The busy rebels captured what King's soldiers they could and left Moreau to his own retreat without pursuit. Yet the faces of the older Colonials struck him, lined, creased, some grizzled with a day's beard. Not a well-dressed man among them. Peasants. Or what you'd call peasants at home. Simple people.

Not so simple after all.

The march went on. Punctuated by brief moments of respite between flashes of carnage, like cards flipped across green felt by a card sharp, swit-swit-swit. Flashing red or black. Black for smoke and ochre, red for seeping blood.

Their second rest period came at a tavern called Munroe House. A formidable two-story structure that looked like two layers of wedding cake, red with white trim. Men from Boston command were spread out over the grounds like broken toys. And you could see through the open windows into the house – soldiers shuffling about, as a pair of colonial tavern keeps hustled back and forth trying to keep everyone supplied with food and drink. And from what Moreau could see, the soldiers were picking the tavern clean.

The Munroe House breather was nearly over, as officers tried to get their men moving again. But the resentment, the weariness had come upon everyone like the cholera, like when slum dwellers drank from the same dirty fountain until everyone was sick. Not to mention the simmering anger for having to look over shoulder every damn second, waiting for a dreaded shot to the gut or the face.

This then, the temporary headquarters of Lieutenant General Percy – and as anyone could plainly see – this general, the only smart one in the lot. The only one thinking ahead. Letting his men rest, scour the place clean of food and drink, even if he had to move them along to allow for all those retreating from Lexington or Concord. Poor sots.

Moreau glanced through an open window into the dining room. The tables and chairs had been swept aside, now served as a makeshift hospital. And now he could see better; scads of dirty and bloody bandages lay about. The entire room a torn scab, an operetta of groaning men.

Moreau spotted Ensign De Bernière – was this the best way off the front? Might there be a better, less dangerous way?

"What about those sketches, D-Bee?"

"Turned them in to Major Toad back in January, and there they vanished."

"But I made copies. Major Toad's maps didn't look like anything we've traversed. I'm betting mine were better."

Moreau tried to remember if any of General Gage's sketches from Major Toad had looked anything like this bit of retreat, run and ruin … but he could not. The trip seemed a faraway time in a distant land of crisp winter mornings and bluebird days with ice shining in the trees.

Now, acrid smoke drifted through the trees, a thick, leafy green hell.

Time to go.

Without respite, their next action came soon enough. The Russell House. Some chroniclers called it the "skirmish." A skirmish.

But skirmish implied some sort of minor engagement. And did not account for the vicious bite of war. Small bodies of troops were fighting up and down the writhing serpent. As if a thousand knife-fights, thug clubs and firearm murders – men angrier than badgers fighting over one thorny gorse bush or another.

The Russell House skirmish, the bloodiest in the lot. The Lieutenant's worm's eye view, close and personal, scalding his mind.

The house stood out because it fronted some trees. Firing came from inside.

Flashes at the open windows, smoke, then sound – flashes from angry, dark eyes. The King's soldiery peppered the housefront but didn't seem to penetrate the walls. The window eyes kept flashing at them. And good men falling.

Nothing to be done here. Without cannon, an assault on the house could go on all day. If they didn't take the house in a few minutes, they'd give up and move on. It would make no difference either way. The road beckoned and mounted now on the good Belle, Moreau kept going.

At another turn he saw the body of a King's man – the arms had been crudely chopped off; the torso impaled upon a wooden fragment of shattered jagged stump.

The colonials managed another flanking movement from a low rise that appeared out of nowhere. Their guns went bang all at once, the smoke rose, and Moreau darted off the road into what he thought was a field. But not a field, a shallow ditch, a trench. The damp rut was crammed with men, some dead, some dying, entangled with the living, a rictus of dead and living love-making.

He felt the shot before he heard it.

No, that wasn't right – he heard the shot before he felt it.

A shoulder bump. Then pain.

And yes, he could walk, stumble along with the others, leading the good Belle by her halter. Stumble along, half blindly; until the houses became closer, more houses, then red brick on both sides of the road, then all were brick. Yes, they'd reached the outskirts of town.

And suddenly it struck him, the futility of an exchange of gunfire. The rebels couldn't win in any strictly military sense but redcoats firing back was like batting a hornet's nest with a flyswatter. You killed a few certainly, but just woke the rest up angry as all get out. Moreau once saw a bear running through the woods with his nose up, covered in prickles of some kind, honeybee, porcupine, nettles … And this is how his troops were dying.

Chapter Eighteen: The Porcupine

Stumbling along with a burning shoulder Moreau came upon his men defaming a body in an alley, mutilating the corpse – turned out to be a woman, dead now, the unknown dead.

Barking harshly at them to leave off.

"Enough of that!"

Soldiers often see dead bodies, sometimes in a tent cot, dying of consumption, sometimes on a town street up against a building, more often than not sprawled out in a wood or a field, among a dozen other dead bodies.

Places where two bodies of men come together. On the outskirts of the town.

This time, a dozen or so rebels had paid the price when standing against a trained formation, looked like a single volley enough to break their ranks. Bodies dropped where they stood or flung over like a discarded doll in the hands of a giant child on the cobblestoned street.

The pale white womanly wrist drew Moreau's eye. A woman among the men. Her tricornered hat flung away and a good bit of her head with it. Unrecognizable. Her luxurious hair, once tightly bound in a bun – now in final disarray. It would take the local people to establish who she belonged to.

He saw no musket by her, but that didn't mean anything. It might have been recovered by either side. Guns were precious, no one left them lying on the ground.

Why was she there?

Fighting? Bringing supplies or ammunition?

A new woman appeared, out from around a brick house – at once, Moreau recognized her. The tavern-keeper, yes, Mary.

Wife of a known rebel. Why so far from her establishment?

What in God's name was she doing here?

The woman coming out to count the dead?

Appearing out of nowhere other women came through the streets, the morning light slanting sideways, their figures, back against the sun, many carrying spades or picks. How many graves to dig today? A trenchful.

If that was really what they were about.

Digging holes among trees was so difficult, roots everywhere needed to be chopped to make a hole. So maybe the women weren't there to dig graves. Not here anyway.

Perhaps they'd come to say a prayer over the dead, to ensure the fallen were given proper Christian rites. If only a few words. Lieutenant Moreau stopped the Hartwell woman and she looked at him, half aghast that he even existed, half in contempt, half in rage and sorrow, so many "halves" there was more of her than any human body could contain.

"Why are you doing this?" Moreau asked her.

And in a moment of blackness, the woman answered: "Why are you?"

And a silence hung in her question.

A silence with an answer he did not know.

The road back to Boston had long ago turned into a writhing, wounded red snake as the Lobsters retreated. First in general order but little by little they twitched and jumped as if wild dogs came out of the brush at every turn, behind every tree, snapping and biting, making the snake turn to fight, when another pair of snapping jaws bared its teeth and sank a fang into unguarded redcoat shanks –

Shudder, twitch, and cry. Leaving the snake, a wounded bloody mess.

Yet Moreau couldn't help imagining another outcome, it rose up in him like bile. The gritty blood lust for revenge. Fantasy better than any reality. How dare the rubes test the righteous order of all things ordained? How dare they throw down the gage.

We shall cut the defiant hand from your wrist.

And pay the butcher's bill.

Now we'll see who is master.

You or me.

In his fevered mind Moreau heard His Majesty's cannonaded ships roar their divine retribution. Letting fly hot iron over Boston rooftops, indiscriminate, random wreckage in final vengeance. White hot cannon balls smashing houses to kindling. Wooden beams to matchwood. Dwellings ablaze. The rim of the town, fired like an ancient burning sacrifice in Dante's hell.

While more murderous balls sailed into the forest beyond the town. Cannon rounds dashing trees to splinters. Rebels and dunclads in the forest taken by surprise. As ball after ball shattered the woods, tearing apart the shivering flesh of countless bodies. The molten iron of each fusillade shimmering into a thousand hot, slashing shards.

But only in Moreau's fevered mind.

For when he reached the final rise and looked down upon Boston harbor a great silence greeted him. A gloomy silence of sleeping artillery and mute ships. A shallow draft landing-barge waited on the shore, with a mass of men waiting to board. A hundred or so, sure to swamp the flatboat if they all embarked. Take two trips at least to ferry the mass of men, and as Moreau walked the good Belle up to the makeshift dock, the mass of soldiers tugged forelocks or saluted his rank. Moving silently out of the way to let him get on the barge first.

But Moreau held up his hand, "No" – calling out clearly – "Embark in order of your arrival. First troops first, second troops second, and so on!"

The men became noticeably relieved, and the murmur round their rank shuddered with quiet approval. As if to say, now here was an officer worth listening to!

The first men mounted the shallow-draft boat across the Charles in quiet order, wounded first, able bodied second. The able men almost too tired to row, but row they did, stroke after stroke, dipping their miserable oars into the miserable water. Across the bay sailors stood by their run-out guns, the gunports open, row after row of gaping mouths on the sides of monstrous ships –

Then faintly, the calls of boatsmen and oarsmen, and faint calls from shipboard, "What happened? What happened? What happened?" Thin calls across the bitter water. Questions that no one from the expedition cared to answer if you hadn't been inland. Leaving instead, the silent mouths of cannon in mute bewilderment.

Lieutenant Moreau dimly recalled from before the expedition – how awful he thought their urine-scented tents on the commons – the muck, the mire, the awful drafty things. But now all he could think of was a tent cot, somewhere, anywhere he could lay down instead of the hard stones of cobblestoned streets. Let him just get there and he would bless the day that tent was raised. Just let him get there and he would bless every stinking soldier who staked every blessed stinking tent.

It struck him now, this bloody, shameful retreat to the safety of Boston, this bitter slog back to the safety of His Majesty's ships of war. And he knew as if for the first and last time, the great and mighty beast his countrymen had woken.

The waiting ships' cannon finally spoke. A useless bombardment sailed into fields and woods and empty space too late. And Moreau knew for certain now that this terrible creature following his men would have the final word. No matter how long delayed or put off. No matter how many British battles won. An appointed reckoning was foretold in the stony African face from the church tower staring down. A black man watching them. No one's slave. No one's property but the knowledgeable, wizened face of a wise man. The face of freedom. A face you'd never mistake for anything but what it was. Strong. Resolute. Inviolate. Promising a debt due with compound interest. An end like no other. The King's final colonial battle lost. Irrevocably. And forever.

"Can I help you, sir?"

The boyish face of one of his own men bobbed before his eye. And suddenly he felt very weak, his legs soft, his breathing ragged.

His young soldier asked again, "Let me help you, sir. We'll take care of the horse." It seemed the good Belle was bleeding. A cut on the strong curve of her hindquarter.

And when the Lieutenant looked at his own hand, he saw he'd been clutching his arm all this long while. And it dawned on him that somewhere along the way, the bridge, the house, the road back, somewhere – he had been struck. Wounded, yes. In his shoulder above the ribs. It suddenly pained him now, and he couldn't breathe.

"Let us help you, Sir."

The reins gently taken from his hands.

And the last thing Moreau remembered before bleeding to faint, the last thing he remembered was the face of that Negro looking down at him. Looking down at him from the North Church. A black face framed in white painted lintels of the bell tower. Sad, wise. Pitiless and cold.

Epilogue: Happy Christmas

December came on wings of spun glass. Cold and white and icy.

Command, in its infinite wisdom abandoned forays into the countryside; content to sit in Boston proper and wait for resupply. Which became its own kind of war, a frigid purgatory. A rebel siege of the town prevented any goods from arriving by land, while Boston harbor allowed deliveries by boat when under royal escort. But supply lines on both sides were stretched and broken in places, and slowly but surely the streets of Boston became barren and hungry.

Life became a slow dance of sniper fire, minor skirmishes, and the desperate scrabble for anything to eat besides fish and oysters. Oyster stew without milk or chicken stock went from monotonous to nauseating. It became obvious to anyone with eyes to see that Boston Town would not last till spring. No ale in the taverns, no wassailing in the narrow streets, no plum pudding, no crown roast – Christmastime became dark and hungry, the sound of dreary hymns seeping like weeping sores from this pew or that.

And so, when all was said and done, desertion found Lieutenant Moreau. Part by design, part by accident. A scrap of newspaper found its way into the barracks, and Moreau managed to read it before folding it carefully to fill the holes in his boot soles. A social notice in The Times of some note.

Fair Meg of Mayfair wedded Knight Bachelor Bontes – Bontesquieu? The full name rubbed out, unreadable. Bontesomebody. In a June wedding of some magnificence.

The only surprise beside an initial pang of jealousy – not that fair Meg had gone her own way, but that after a few breaths, he cared so little. Whatever reason he might have had to return to his clammy homeland had suddenly vanished.

And so, one darkening December afternoon Moreau found himself walking the faithful Belle out Boston Neck to Roxbury. A desertion born from desolation and ennui. The profound boredom of knowing nothing was going to change, except dwindling supplies, a bout of barracks-cough and the irretrievable loss of purpose. Truly, the Army and Navy's royal occupation had lost its way.

Back again walking the Menotomy Road, only this time not in uniform, no longer a redcoat. Walking at dusk so as not to be recognized, blue cloaked, leading the faithful Belle by her halter.

A mile or so out from Boston, Moreau overtook another lonely traveler, slower than himself. A bent Negro trudging along, pulling a handcart, packed with goods, but covered with an oilcloth. Cargo a mystery. Even in the dark, cold night, the man huffed and puffed, dragging his burden along.

"Here now," the Lieutenant addressed the fellow. And his voice cut the cold air like a knife. The bent Negro looked at him with a dagger of fear and suspicion. Then at the faithful Belle with a touch of envy.

"Here now," Moreau said again. "Let us hitch my good and faithful horse to that hand cart and make your burden lighter."

The bent Negro stopped in his tracks, with a sigh of exhaustion and relief and replied, "That Sir, would be mighty welcome."

"Her name is Belle," Moreau told the man, as they hitched the traces to the back saddle rings on the cart with an extra coil of leather straps.

"Well, she be good enough for me," the black man replied. "Obliged to you, Sir."

The night being what it was, a kind of equalizer on the status of men; the dark itself a great leveler of rank and position. It occurred to neither man to measure the other's hierarchy in the scheme of things.

The horse was hitched but at the last moment she snorted and shook her head and a small piece of the canvas cover slid away. Clear now what the handcart contained. The dull gleam of gun barrels on wooden stocks – muskets. And by their immaculate condition, brand new ones. The black man took a breath, but let it out smooth. Unafraid. Moreau slapped the oilcloth back in place.

"All right then."

They went on. And for an hour the night was quiet. Until the dread sound of horses trotting came back at them from up ahead. Perhaps the game was up. A troop of three red-coated cavalry men appeared before them like the Final Judgement. And the handcart, horse, and two men ground to a halt. Two of the riders passed by without slowing down, but one tarried. Inspection?

"Well, what have you to say for yourself," the cavalryman demanded.

Neither Moreau nor Cuddy knew what to say.

"C-can't imagine," Moreau stuttered. "'Good Evening', is the best I can do. Sir."

The redcoat snorted. "Let's have a look, shall we?" and twisted his horse about, preparing to dismount. "You then, let's see!"

Moreau didn't immediately uncover the hand-cart, instead he chose a delay.

"Perhaps we can give you something for your trouble," Moreau fished into his purse and the sound of coins clinked. The redcoat's eyes lit with greed.

But in a moment of saving grace, voices rang out from his fellows down the road.

"Singian, come along! No time for bribes!"

The horse swung around again and the sound of recoated hooves faded down the road.

Lieutenant Moreau and Mister Cuddy approached the Hartwell Tavern as night finally fell. He brought the faithful Belle to the open barn door. Entering in the dark, and suddenly stopped by a voice –

"There's a charge you know. Feed and water, we have some alfalfa – that which the Lobsters didn't eat themselves."

The voice, from a dark figure standing in an empty stall. And the former Lieutenant recognized her at once. Mary Hartwell. The strong mock of hair, the laced bodice, the all-business stoic and tavern keep.

"Glad to pay. Her name is Belle, she's a good horse."

Mary touched Belle's hind quarter and Belle's hide twitched as Mary's fingers grazed the scar.

"Saber cut?"

The Lieutenant didn't know what to say. Moreau didn't answer. Then after long moments, "Must have been."

"You were there?"

"Aye." That day was long and very confused. I saw you. We called you the Soldiers' Widow. You said the prayer. You were at the graves along the road."

"Yes. Like you I was on that road all day."

"A very long day." He unstrapped the girth under good Belle.

"You are red-coated no more?" Her eyes questioning his leather and dun garments. Again, as if to be sure, "Red-coated no more?"

He unslung his bedroll and leather dispatch case off the pommel and slung the saddle over a saddle mount, bedroll, leather case and all.

"I am red-coated no more," he answered. "So, if you take me for a spy, best call your husband to arrest me. We can tell everyone I brought it on myself."

The woman nodded her head as if surmising as much.

"Well, come in the tavern then. We'll take you in for the night. We can talk. And perhaps tomorrow send you on a proper path."

A proper path. How could he ever find a proper path again? Deserter, turncoat, the lowest of the low. The man who led His Majesty's troops to a defeat. Then crawled back to the barracks with wounded men leaving the dead ones behind. For a split second he saw a fragment of that horrid day again – the despairing face of Corporal Cummins cradling the head of Sergeant Bates, rocking back and forth as though holding a baby, and crying. Wiping the wet from his face before abandoning the body and making for home.

Mary Hartwell offered him a clean rag from the trim of her bodice.

His own face wet too. He took the ragged handkerchief and mopped his eyes.

"Come inside then," the woman told him. "It's over now. You're done. One way or the other, I don't think there'll be a rope for you."

Acknowledgements

It's important to thank Stephen Schwab and the Museum of the American Revolution for their great help in writing this book.

Also, Nancy Mosher for her critical eye and challenging questions, and my wife, Maxine for her bottomless patience with a husband whose mantra ricocheted between "I can't talk now, " and "Did you say something?"

And finally Bob Ackerman, for that critical editorial twist that made the book what it is today.

Keith Korman is an American literary agent and novelist. Over the years he has represented many nationally known clients through his family's agency, Raines & Raines. The agency is most noted for representing the following books: *The Detective, Deliverance, Die Hard, Cruising, My Dog Skip, How to Eat Fried Worms* and *Forrest Gump*. Korman's novels include *Secret Dreams, Banquo's Ghosts* (with Rich Lowry), and *End Time* -- updated under the title *Teahouse of the Hidden Moon*.

www.ingramcontent.com/pod-product-compliance
Lightning Source LLC
Chambersburg PA
CBHW030613310726
48979CB00003B/700

* 9 7 8 1 9 5 7 5 8 6 4 4 1 *